Praise for

I0616873

A.J. Llewellyn and Serena Yates

...fun, witty, and light wrapped up in the suspense of strange happenings... The Cake is rip-roaring, roller coaster ride from the beginning... I can't wait to see what they come up with for the second book in the Elemental Superpower series
~ *Dark Divas Reviews*

...The personalities of both men are interesting and a little bit quirky...left me wanting a cupcake and a glass of milk the entire time I was reading... Good choice, AJ and Serena...
~ *Fallen Angel Reviews*

...one of the most entertaining books I've read in a long time. It has everything — romance, intrigue, humor... If you enjoy a tender story in which love and justice prevail, then chances are, you will enjoy 'The Cake'. ~ *Queer Magazine Online*

Elemental Superpowers

THE CAKE

A.J. LLEWELLYN and SERENA YATES

Elemental Superpowers: The Cake
ISBN # 978-0-85715-429-3
©Copyright A.J. Llewellyn and Serena Yates 2011
Cover Art by Posh Gosh ©Copyright 2011
Interior text design by Claire Siemaszkiewicz
Total-E-Bound Publishing

Published in 2011 by Total-E-Bound Publishing, Think Tank, Ruston Way,
Lincoln, LN6 7FL, United Kingdom.

Manufactured in the USA.

THE CAKE

Dedication

To all those who share our passion for cupcakes.

"Beneath those stars is a universe of gliding monsters."
~ Herman Melville

Chapter One

God, it was hopeless. He'd prepared what he thought was a damned good class on advanced criminal procedure, but the blank faces staring back at Phillip Sedgwick indicated otherwise. He scanned the body language of his thirty students. They all seemed to lean to the right, as if any moment their bodies would airlift en masse, hurling their way out through the doors. Well, he was bored too, but come on, he was a cool guy. He had smarts. He had charisma...didn't he?

It was annoying as hell. Half of the students and their inane questions drove him up the wall, the other half looked so uninterested he wasn't sure they were even alive. Granted, not everyone here would become a judge or legislator, but he'd hoped his second-year class would have gained a more advanced understanding of at least *some* of the concepts he tried to teach. He'd also, apparently mistakenly, presumed they had a higher level of interest in the elective course.

In desperation, his gaze fell on the girl in the third row. She openly read a book that he knew, from its colourful binding, had absolutely nothing to do with the subject matter. It probably wasn't even a textbook related to the law at all. The guy sitting beside her elbowed her, his gaze meeting Phillip's. The girl kept reading, oblivious to all the attention now focussed on her.

Phillip felt a trickle of sweat bead at his collar.

Oh, my God! My body's leaning towards the door, too!

He straightened his back. No, he didn't want to stay in the stuffy room any more than they did, but since the new college rules clamped down on using air conditioning in the spring and none of the windows opened, they would all have to suffer.

Outside, San Francisco beckoned. He ached to feel the breeze he could see ruffling the leaves on the trees, wanting its cooling action on his skin. Below that, he saw green grass and a few students barefoot, lying on their backs. He swallowed down a pang of jealousy. *Callow youths*…if only they knew how lucky they were.

With the silence having gone on for too long and half of the class staring at him, he had no choice. He had to take control. Besides, he'd damn well played to much tougher crowds and won.

Phillip left his desk at the front of the room and strode up the stairs on the left side of the lecture room, stopping by the girl still immersed in her book.

"Anything you care to share with the rest of us?" he asked, hands on hips.

Too late, he saw the title: *The Sex Life of the Foot and Shoe.* Great, just great.

She looked up, blinking. A few kids smothered smiles. A couple of them giggled. She had the grace to look embarrassed. Phillip walked back to his desk, leaning on the podium, and waited.

"Um…yeah. It's interesting. It…well, it's about the history of shoe design…and why people wear certain types of shoes."

"And it relates to advanced criminal procedure…how?"

The girl chewed at her lip. "Well, it says you can tell a lot about people by the shoes they choose to wear."

"Really. And what do my shoes tell you about me?"

Her gaze never left his face. "You wear boots. You're sexually confident, inclined to think highly of yourself. According to the book, since yours are never scuffed, you're probably great in the sack."

The class burst into laughter. Phillip, mortified, took a deep breath and hoped his embarrassment didn't show. He did what any good circus master would do. He used the situation to his advantage.

"You see," he said, when the laughter subsided, "a good criminal investigator uses all the tools he has at his disposal to his advantage, however limited they might be. Did anyone here see the movie *The Silence of the Lambs*?"

Several hands shot up into the air. He warmed to his subject now that he had the attention of the entire room.

"When Clarice Starling goes to the prison to visit Hannibal Lecter, she knows everything about him. He knows nothing about her. With the benefit of *only* his powers of observation and the evidence before him, he starts with her shoes. Does anyone remember what he says to her?"

Again, several hands shot up and he picked out a guy who had been half asleep for most of their hour together.

"He said her handbag was expensive, but she was wearing cheap shoes."

"Very good. So what is the point he is trying to make?"

He pointed to another student, who said, "The shoes spoil the effect of the rest of the confident, worldly image she's trying to convey."

"Exactly." Phillip glanced across the room at them all. "He was trying to embarrass the woman in that scene, but let's look at it from an investigator's point of view. What does it tell you about a woman if she carries an expensive bag but wears inferior shoes?"

The girl who had started the whole conversation in the first place was bouncing up and down in her seat, hand up in the air. Phillip pointed to her.

"She's not vain. The bag carries the things that are important to her. Her case load, her cell phone...whatever. The shoes are simple tools that get her from point A to point B."

"Very good point." Phillip nodded to another guy. "Look at the person next to you. What do his shoes tell you?"

The guy looked down. "A close relationship with pizza sauce and dog shit, and a very poor one with hygiene."

Everyone laughed. The whole class ended up on their feet, studying shoes. Phillip congratulated himself as the bell rang. This hadn't been a total loss after all.

"Okay then, your papers on the relationship between mental states and criminal responsibility are due by next Wednesday."

"I'm going over to Payless," one of the girls said to her friends as they walked out. "I gotta buy me some confident shoes."

The room emptied at a leisurely pace. That was pretty cool.

"Great class, Professor Sedgwick," somebody called out as he assembled his papers and slid them into his briefcase.

Good. Teaching law at UC San Francisco may be a good cover, since nobody suspected a professor to be involved in anything out of the ordinary, but, damn it, he did have some pride in his job. Even the fake one.

His new employer required he teach at least one course each semester, for recruiting purposes. He snorted. From what he'd seen of them so far, he wouldn't recruit any of these people if his life depended on it.

He was just as eager as his students to get outside into the brilliant late April sunshine. He breathed a sigh of relief when he finally made it, standing on the steps for a moment to inhale the fresh air. The most important question now was whether he'd have time for a coffee and a cupcake at the bakery on Fulton Street, right across from the campus. He'd wanted to pay the store a visit ever since he'd discovered it when he first moved to the city.

Its cosy-looking eating area taunted him, inviting him to sit down and take a break for a few minutes. He could smell the cakes from here. He paused to get a whiff of what they'd been working on. Damn it, they'd just baked the strawberry shortcake flavour. He knew his nose was right because the sign out front advertised the changing daily offerings confirming his theory. His mouth watered. The entire faculty and most of the students were obsessed with those cupcakes. At least they got to eat them. So far he'd had no luck.

When his phone rang he sighed. It looked like today was going to be no different. No cupcakes for him. Checking caller ID confirmed it was his assistant, Declan North, the man who made the office part of his life run smoothly. Arden, Bainbridge, Chinook and Damek was a large law firm which had been a successful cover for lawyers like him for generations. They paid extremely well, but expected utter dedication, day and night. There was no point trying to hide, so he flipped open his phone.

"What can I do for you, Declan?" He glanced towards Fabulous Cupcakes one last time, but started walking towards his car.

"Good afternoon to you, too, sir." Declan sounded almost affronted. "I'm calling to let you know that something extremely urgent has come up and that you're expected back at the office as soon as *humanly* possible."

"It's always urgent, Declan." He thumbed open his car door, dumped the briefcase behind his seat and got in, closing the door behind him with an audible thunk. Dammit, he'd really wanted that cupcake.

"Yes, sir." Declan sighed. "I'm just doing my job."

"I know. You're very good at it, too." The man was too efficient for his own good, but Phillip needed someone like him to keep an eye on the pesky little details, especially since he seemed to be spending a lot more time out of the office than in his previous jobs. His new employer expected their employees to be far more hands-on than Phillip liked.

"Thank you, sir." Declan coughed. "Can I tell Mr. Arden that you'll be here in half an hour?"

"I'll do my best." He put on his seatbelt and started the engine. "Traffic permitting, I should be there on time."

"Thank you, sir." Declan hung up.

* * * *

Phillip spent the next twenty minutes making his way back to the downtown office, trying to figure out what was so urgent this time. He still took wrong streets even when he used his on-board GPS system. That was mostly because he tended to mute it and miss vital turns. With so many one-way streets near the vicinity of Union Square, it meant doubling back many times. He hated the bossy female voice on his system, but he turned her on now and followed her instructions. Obviously, nobody had told her that men were genetically wired not to follow directions.

He mused on the work issue. There weren't any big cases he was involved in, so it must be something new. He mentally rubbed his hands. Anything was better than teaching at the college, and with any luck he'd be so busy with this new case that a colleague would take over his class. It had happened once or twice before, so he had high hopes.

Panhandlers groped at his windows at the corner of Market Street. He was forced to move forward with the fast-changing lights. The hunger in the men's eyes made him feel guilty about pining for cupcakes.

Man, he'd never noticed so many shoe stores before. Almost every second store sold shoes. Ugg of Australia...cheap shoes...fancy shoes...two-for-the-price-of-one shoes. Some woman called Ria had a gigantic store that reeked of money. Men's shoes... Man, there was even a hospital for shoes! Who the hell was buying all these shoes?

What did it convey? He shook these random thoughts from his mind.

After he parked and made it to the senior partner's office on the twelfth floor, he was still on time. He almost bounced with anticipation. The older secretary looked over her steel-rimmed glasses and shot him a disapproving look. It brought him back to reality and he curbed his nervous energy before entering the office.

Mr. Ignatius Arden was a power to be reckoned with. His office was decorated in deep browns and reds, with orange and yellow highlights. There was no denying which of the four superpower sources he represented. The man sat behind a mahogany desk that looked brand new. It was empty. Phillip longed to see a piece of paper, something on it. Mr. Arden placed an open file onto it, holding a fountain pen in his hand. As if it was an afterthought, he conjured a notepad onto the table's smooth, polished surface.

Show-off. If I did that, I'd be reprimanded.

His boss was even more organised than Declan, and now checked his watch. His chestnut hair was cut extremely short and he frowned when he looked up.

Phillip couldn't resist taking a peek at the man's shoes. He wondered what the author of *The Sex Life of the Foot and Shoe* would say about the spit-shined tan leather shoes with their elegant laces and tassels instead of the traditional aglets on the end.

Holy cow, how come I never noticed those before? What do they say about him? He's quirky? Autocratic? Egotistical? Is he good in bed?

"Something wrong, Mr. Sedgwick?"

"Oh, no. No, sir." He lifted his gaze from the floor.

"I'm glad you could make it, Mr. Sedgwick." Mr. Arden sat back in his leather chair and smiled. "I have quite the new assignment for you, should you choose to accept it."

Phillip nodded. As if he'd have a choice. He wasn't exactly planning to make a CLM—a career limiting move—this early in his employment, if ever. Turning down an assignment was never a clever idea, and in fact could be downright dangerous considering the kind of powers his bosses had.

"It has come to our owners' attention that there has been an extreme, completely illegal and consistent misuse of superpowers by one of the inhabitants of this city." Mr. Arden looked at the file for a second. "It has lasted several years and the perpetrator has not reacted to either our warnings or to our request to cease and desist."

"That is incredibly short-sighted of him." *More like downright suicidal.*

"It is indeed." Mr. Arden closed the file. "We want you to make his acquaintance in whatever way you think appropriate, find out what's going on and come back to us with a recommendation on how to proceed. Obviously, we want to prosecute. You have one week to collect the necessary evidence and create an iron-clad case for us."

One week wasn't much, but he supposed it could be done. Some initial research into the man's background would already have been completed, judging by the thickness of the file, so he could get right to the 'get to know him' stage. He nodded. Yes, it was possible.

"What is your answer, Mr. Sedgwick?" Mr. Arden looked surprisingly tense, as if a lot was riding on Phillip's decision.

"I accept the assignment." He leant forward to hold his hand out for the file.

When Mr. Arden handed it to him, he glanced at the one-page summary of key facts stapled to the front. The suspect was one Mr. Daine Paradis, owner of Fabulous Cupcakes, 2200 Fulton Street, San Francisco.

Fuck me! He was going to get his cupcakes after all. He pushed himself away from Mr. Arden's desk, his mind already on flavour choices and icing.

"Mr. Sedgwick?"

Phillip looked up from his file. "Yes, sir?"

"Just so you know…all my lovers have always said I am the best fuck they ever had."

* * * *

"Yes, ma'am. The vegan cupcakes really are vegan."

The thin woman squinted at the items on display with a level of mistrust normally reserved for criminals. Whilst she tried to make up her mind, Daine stared at the never-ending line of customers stretching from the sales counter all the way to the bakery door. There were harried business people and chatting students with backpacks, housewives in a rush and hand-holding couples of all ages.

"And what does SF mean?" She jabbed at a flag in one of the trays of cupcakes.

"Sugar-free."

"Are they any good?"

He frowned. "Good? They're fabulous!"

That drew a few laughs from the waiting throng, but Daine panicked when one couple left the store in frustration. He poked his head around the kitchen door.

"Antonio!"

"Si, señor." Antonio, one of his new bakers, came out with a huge tray laden with generous samples of hot chocolate cupcakes in tiny white paper cups. He also had a pocketful of fifty-cents-off coupons good for seven days, another incentive for anyone who stuck around. Hot chocolate was the flavour selected for the following day. Daine could tell by the murmur of approval he'd made the right decision. It made him feel good to know everyone wanted one of the unique creations that Fabulous Cupcakes had become well-known for over the last few years.

Unfortunately, it didn't look like he'd be able to take a break any time soon.

"Are those samples vegan?" the woman asked, a hopeful look on her face.

"I'm sorry, no."

"Sugar-free?"

He grinned. "Sorry."

She didn't hide her disappointment. "Well, if you're sure about the lemon bar cupcakes, I'll take one. I want the one with lots of lemon frosting." She looked at him, her expression stern. "But if I have any issues with it at all, you — or rather your boss — will be hearing from me."

I am the boss, lady. Daine looked a lot younger than his twenty-eight years, or so people told him, but she probably wouldn't believe him on that point. She probably wouldn't believe he was the owner of the bakery, either. There was no time to get into a pointless fight anyway.

"Of course, ma'am." Daine used his favourite antique silver tongs to pick up the single cupcake which had taken the woman five minutes to choose.

"Not that one. That one." She pointed to one that had slightly more icing.

"Would you like to eat it here, or have it to go?"

She wagged a finger at him. "You'll charge me extra to eat it here, won't you?"

"No. I just want to know if I should put it in a box for you to take it home or if you'll be eating it now."

He wished to God he had one kitchen hand who could speak English well enough to help out behind the counter for a few minutes.

"I'll have it to go," she said, counting dimes on to the counter.

Why is it that the people who buy a single cupcake always take ten years to pick one? And then pay in small change?

He opened a fresh box, squeezed a dollop of butter cream on the bottom with the pastry bag and popped the cupcake on top to secure it. He taped the sides shut, relieved to be done. He felt as if he'd aged a decade during this one, single transaction.

Silvio, his best baker when the guy wasn't plagued with dental problems and immigration hearings, bustled out with a fresh load of red velvet cupcakes. Half the tray had the traditional cream cheese frosting, the other half was covered in dark chocolate, which had turned out to be a surprising hit.

"How are the others coming along?" Daine tried to keep the fear out of his voice. If he panicked, Silvio panicked. The flour-smeared baker gave him a thumbs-up and hustled back to the kitchen.

Antonio came back in from outside the store, emboldened by the hearty response to his samples.

"I help?" he asked in broken English.

"*Si*, yes," Daine said, relieved.

Antonio had obviously watched Daine often enough to know that he started on the left-hand side of the store and let people point out the cakes they wanted from behind the counter's window display. He took up some tongs, placing each cupcake carefully on a tray balanced in his other hand. Daine was so sick of eating cupcakes, he'd ceased to see ruined cakes as fringe benefits. Antonio was mortified when one of his cupcakes fell on the tray, the immaculate icing becoming smeared.

"Don't worry," Daine said. "You can eat it." He mimed eating to the baker.

Antonio's face lit up. He left the tray on the counter and ran back to the kitchen with his prize.

"Not now!" Daine shouted. For the next ten minutes, he filled boxes, retrieved pre-ordered party packs of mini cupcakes and made sure somebody was chopping up more samples in the kitchen.

Every time he looked up, the line was still long. Of all the days for Cairo, his only assistant in the store and genius icing maker in the kitchen, to develop some strange malady. He adored Cairo Rhodes, but didn't adore her tendency to become sick right before a holiday weekend. The next few customers seemed to want one of everything and, with forty-six flavours to choose from, Daine was rushed off his feet.

He loved the children who came in because they were dazzled by the icing colours and imaginative toppings Cairo chose, but for some reason, today, even the kids made Daine want to scream.

Everyone seemed to have complicated orders or to want extra fast service. Well, it was lunchtime after all.

The only people who were more relaxed were the couples who had sat down to enjoy their treats at one of the many cast-iron tables set up throughout the shop. They all looked so much in love that it hurt. Daine wanted to have what they had, but he was much too shy to approach anyone, never mind another man. His uncle would kill him if he ever found out Daine was gay. Who knew what might have happened if his parents still talked to him, but that was a useless thought. They hadn't spoken for years.

When he looked up from completing the sale of a mini selection, he was confronted with the best-looking man who'd ever entered his bakery.

"Ooh," one of the little kids squealed. "Mom! The root beer float cupcake is like having a party in my mouth!"

This put a smile on Daine's face. As did the handsome hottie standing in front of him. He was at least six-foot-four, had deep brown eyes the colour of bitter chocolate and short, liquorice-black hair, which the perfect topping for his milk-chocolate coloured skin. Daine couldn't help it. He always thought in terms of food.

The yummy man's shoulders were wide, stretching to capacity the white T-shirt he wore, and his smile was unusual in the hectic atmosphere of early afternoon.

Jerking his thumb over his shoulder, Mr. Gorgeous said, "Sounds like your cupcakes are a big hit. Is it always this busy?"

Mr. Gorgeous didn't seem to be in any hurry at all.

"Yes. Always...around lunchtime." *Way to go, slick.* Daine desperately wished he could think of something clever to say.

"So now isn't a good time for me to ask you for an explanation about all these wonderful looking confections?" Mr. Gorgeous tilted his head. Going for the innocent look didn't really work for him, but Daine didn't mind. The high cheek bones, straight nose and strong jaw fascinated him.

"Strawberry shortcake!" he shrieked. *Real slick, Daine. Man, what the hell is wrong with me?*

The man was just too gorgeous.

"You have any dietary concerns?" he asked.

"No...not really. Shoe leather doesn't appeal, but strawberry shortcake sounds good. It's the flavour of the day, isn't it?"

Yes. And I want to lick your cherry.

"Yes, it is. And here's Antonio with some samples."

His new baker was back, his face smeared in blue and green bubblegum icing.

"You like?" Antonio thrust the tray right under the gorgeous man's nose.

"I'll let you know in a few seconds." Mr. Gorgeous took one.

"Sorry," Daine said. For the first time in months, he wanted an encounter with another man that took longer than a few seconds and didn't involve the words, *You want coffee with that?* Not that he was going to get more than that. Not that he'd *ever* got what he wanted from a man he was interested in. He shook his head. This wasn't the time to reminisce about his failed relationships.

"Hey, no need to apologise, especially when your cupcakes taste this good."

Mr. Gorgeous took a second sample. The lady with the vegan requirements was back and helping herself to a non-vegan sample. Oh well, if she wanted to flirt with gastro-intestinal distress…

"It's just that I haven't been inside a bakery in a long time and could do with some extra instruction," Mr. Gorgeous said.

Is this guy flirting with me? And why the hell does he keep looking over the counter? I swear he's staring at my feet…wait! Maybe he's looking at the floor? Maybe he thinks we have vermin. Holy crap! What if he's a health inspector?

Daine took a deep breath and smiled.

"I need to get something special for a friend and all I know is that he likes cupcakes. What would you recommend I get for him?" Mr. Gorgeous tilted his head, looking adorably clueless.

"If it's a special occasion I would recommend a bouquet, but you'd have to come by and pick it up later. Just take your time picking out the cupcake sizes, the flavour and, of course, how many." Daine handed Mr. Gorgeous the catalogue, wishing he could be the friend his newest customer was lavishing so much attention on.

Mr. Gorgeous stepped aside, flicking through the extensive information as Daine helped more customers.

He turned away from the crowd, busy tucking paper into a box separating four chocolate salted-caramel cupcakes, and when he was done he caught Mr. Gorgeous leaning over the counter again.

I was right! He's staring at my feet. He glanced down at his shoes. They were clean. How weird. Why did Mr. Gorgeous keep staring at his feet?

Everyone oohed and aahed when a fresh batch of the house special, the Fabulous Cupcake, came out of the kitchen.

"We need chocolate and coconut cupcakes," Daine told Antonio as the baker headed back to the kitchen.

Daine began to panic. They seemed to be taking their time icing cupcakes. He glimpsed Silvio lounging outside the kitchen door, smoking. State law said he had to be twelve feet from the building. Damn!

At least he had a dozen of the Fabulous for now.

"What's in that?" Mr. Gorgeous asked.

"Raspberry butter cream, raspberry preserve in the middle and a layer of fresh raspberry cream under the icing."

Mr. Gorgeous returned his attention to the laminated brochure.

Daine boxed up the last of his red velvet cupcakes for a customer who kept tapping his credit card on the glass counter top, as if this would hurry things along. Daine could have told him it wouldn't. He gritted his teeth and moved as fast as he could. If he could tell people one thing about buying food, it would be: *Never piss off your food server. They could spit in your meal…or worse.*

He ran the customer's credit card, but it was declined. As the customer handed him one card after another, Daine swiped them all. He suddenly saw the word *stolen* flashing on the readout on his credit card machine. The guy must have realised, because he took off, a dozen cupcakes with a street value of thirty-six dollars in his red-hot hands.

Mr. Gorgeous sauntered after the guy. Daine wanted to tell him not to get involved, but he was already gone. He returned seconds later. Daine and the woman now waiting for service at the counter gasped when Mr. Gorgeous handed back the box of stolen cakes.

"How'd you do that?" Daine was impressed.

"Can I buy those?" the woman asked.

"Do you want them?" Daine asked his knight in shining armour.

"I'm sure they're very nice, but I have my heart set on a dozen strawberry shortcakes. That's sort of like a dozen red roses, right?"

Daine nodded, trying very hard not to show his disappointment. This *friend* must be a very close one to deserve such a wonderful gift.

He rang up the sale for the woman in front of him, relieved when Antonio came out with fresh strawberry shortcake cupcakes. He had a ring of pink cream around his mouth.

Mr. Gorgeous turned his smouldering gaze back to Daine. "While I'm here, I'd love to have a cup of coffee and whatever cupcake you recommend."

Daine stopped writing up the baking order for the dozen cupcake bouquet and stared at the object of his admiration. Mr. Gorgeous was going to sit here and have coffee? He was going to allow himself to be ogled as Daine worked? How was Daine supposed to get anything done with *him* in the store?

Mr. Gorgeous frowned. "Are you okay?"

"Yeah, I'm fine, thank you." Daine felt the heat flush his much too white skin. God, he'd been caught daydreaming like a teenager. "Sorry."

"Don't worry. I was just wondering if these are all made from your own recipes?" Mr. Gorgeous licked his lips and Daine was mesmerised.

I can't remember. What was the question again?

"Um…yes." *Please kiss me.* The man wanted to know about recipes. "We have a few basic recipes. People sort of expect some of the traditional cakes. We have dozens of specials that are our own creations, including seasonal varieties, like eggnog and Christmas pudding for the holidays…pumpkin for Thanksgiving—"

"I'm looking at your monthly brochure. It's staggering. Do people really buy the pancake and bacon cupcakes?"

"Sure they do." Daine tried not to bristle at the suggestion of otherwise.

"Can I have one of those, please?" Mr. Gorgeous pointed at a batch of newly-arrived cherry pie cupcakes.

"These are my favourites." Daine would have given the man anything for another smile like that.

"I like the lattice top…like a tiny cherry pie. I have to have one." Mr. Gorgeous stared and licked his lips again.

Let me lick those for you.

It looked like the man was at least as much into cupcakes as Daine. And that was a lot… Suddenly Daine was rediscovering his love for his own creations.

"Would you like to have a seat while I make a fresh pot of coffee?"

"Okay."

Daine plated the cupcake and handed it to him. "It's on the house, for…you know…rescuing the goodies."

"Think nothing of it." Mr. Gorgeous took the offered plate with a smile and walked off to find a table. Man, the back view was just as perfect as the front.

Daine shook his head and forced his attention back on his job. He rang up sale after sale, the line of new customers still as long as ever. During a brief break in foot traffic, Mr. Gorgeous came back with his credit card to pay for his bouquet.

So, Mr. Gorgeous had a name. Phillip Sedgwick. Mr. Gorgeous suited him much better.

He watched the man pull his wallet from the back pocket of his pants. It caused the front to strain across a considerable bulge that made Daine's mouth water.

Man, I need to get a life.

He poured the guy some coffee and watched as Mr. Gorgeous took his cup over to his table near the window. Was he going to see him again? He was sure the man had never been to his store before. He would have remembered if he had.

Daine sighed, turning towards the next customer before he could make a fool of himself. The man hadn't shown any sign of being interested. Daine had to stop mooning after strangers. If he was destined to remain alone, the least he could do was bear his fate with dignity.

Chapter Two

"More hands-on research at the store tomorrow, sir?" Declan's face scrunched into disapproval.

"Yes, as a matter of fact." Phillip hadn't succeeded in more than making contact during his visit earlier that day.

The delectable Daine had been far too busy serving other customers. As far as he could tell, the man worked hard and ran a tight ship for someone who was under-staffed and very stressed at the busiest time of day. He hadn't wanted to make his interest too obvious by hanging around the store longer than was normal for a dine-in customer. But he was sure there was more he could find out, given time and opportunity.

"I have to say, his cupcake was the best thing I ever had in my mouth," Phillip said. What had that little kid said in the store? Like a party. Yes, it was.

Declan laughed. "Thanks for the bouquet. The strawberry shortcake cupcakes were the best. The cream frosting was so good I even licked it off the tissue in the box." He glanced up and down the corridor. "And if you ever tell anyone I said that, I'll viciously deny it."

Phillip grinned. "Understood."

He couldn't help peering around the desk to check Declan's shoes. Timberlands. That conveyed absolutely nothing to Phillip. He'd tried several times to see what Daine Paradis had been wearing behind his shop counter. He thought he'd glimpsed brand new running shoes. What did that suggest?

Man. Why am I thinking about the guy? He is a suspect. I need to find proof of his illegal activities…

"I may be spending a lot of time over at the bakery." He needed to focus on the job at hand.

"Certainly, sir. I'll be holding the fort here, then."

"Thank you." Not that he expected his assistant to do anything else. What had got into the man? "I'll be going straight there tomorrow morning, so don't expect me in the office until the afternoon."

"Will you let me know if your plans change?" Declan looked up at him from under his lashes.

"I will." Something was definitely going on. Maybe his assistant was afraid of getting bored? "While I'm gone, I want you to do some more research into the background and family history of Mr. Paradis, please. The usual details."

"Yes, sir." Declan perked up.

That was it, the man was afraid of being bored. Problem solved, Phillip made his way to the gym one floor below, where he worked out harder than usual in the hopes that exhaustion would help him forget about Daine Paradis.

As he rowed the oars on the canoe machine, he thought about Daine. The man was a few inches shorter than him, with a medium build and an underlying wiry strength that called to Phillip. He didn't look a day over eighteen years old, but was actually twenty-eight and had run the family business for over five years. His big, dark green eyes and long blond hair in its neat ponytail gave him an angelic appearance. He even had dimples when he smiled, and he clearly liked to smile.

At the end of a gruelling two-hour workout, he was still thinking about Daine. He took a quick shower before driving to his apartment. What was it about the man that fascinated him so much? He was a suspected criminal, for heaven's sake.

He picked up some takeout Thai from the King of Thai on Union, found his way home—eventually—and sat down on his sofa, switching on the TV. He gobbled his peanut and tofu spaghetti. It was his addiction. *This would make a great cupcake! What the heck am I thinking? I wonder what Daine's doing now?* He checked his watch. Daine was probably still working.

Phillip reached for his peach and lemon iced tea. Damn! He'd left it at the restaurant. He was never this absent-minded. He had to get a grip. He sucked on a long strand of spaghetti as he watched some guy called Billy the Exterminator wrestling a twelve-foot boa constrictor in a New Orleans backyard.

He stared in shocked silence as the boa coiled itself around the exterminator's arm, trying to squeeze the life out of him. Billy screamed. Phillip wasn't sure if it was all for show. Billy explained to his TV audience how you could tell a venomous snake from a non-venomous one.

"A venomous snake has slitty, snake-like eyes. See this one? It has round eyes. He wouldn't bite you. He'll just squeeze you to death."

Once the beast was secured in a massive, plastic bucket, Billy spoke to the camera.

"I think he's one of the forgotten victims of Hurricane Katrina. He's obviously hungry, but weak. He hasn't eaten for a while. I'm going to relocate him to a wildlife rescue service that'll fatten him up in no time."

Billy grinned, looking insanely happy about his creepy, weird-ass job.

* * * *

Daine accepted the carton of takeout Antonio offered him. The peanut smell intoxicated him, improving his mood. It also dispelled his initial disappointment. He liked Thai food well enough, but he'd had his heart set on pizza. Antonio and Silvio had overridden his wishes, even though he'd paid for the takeout order. He poked through the cartons, impressed with the fragrant offerings. He'd heard the King of Thai had the best noodles and so far he hadn't tasted a single one. It was well after eight o'clock, but they'd just closed the bakery doors.

Each man pulled up a chair at the kitchen table where cupcakes were iced and decorated all day long. Somebody hammered on the bakery window. Though Daine, Silvio and Antonio were secluded from view, being in the kitchen, they all froze.

Whoever was at the door kept trying the handle.

"It's locked. We're closed," Daine muttered under his breath. He spooned some noodles onto his plate.

"You don't think it's Immigration, do you?" Silvio asked.

"No, I don't. And besides, you have a work permit now, remember?"

Silvio smiled. "*Si*."

Daine tried not to grimace. Silvio had a mouth full of gold teeth. He seemed to think there was some status in all that metal. Maybe he was right. He had a running stream of breathless women parading in and out of the kitchen all day…and a few kids sprinkled in for good measure. He'd tried to tell Silvio that if he set aside his hard-earned money for his green card instead of buying teeth he'd be a legal resident in no time. Daine had sponsored his entire immigrant kitchen staff for their work papers. Able-bodied Americans could bake and sift and chop and clean, but apparently they didn't want to. Daine was surprised how many immigrants were happy to take anything that involved a few bucks.

They turned up daily. Sometimes he had work for them, sometimes he didn't. He liked hiring people who wanted to work and weren't afraid of long hours. Though San Francisco was officially a sanctuary city, Daine was a by-the-book guy. He wanted no trouble with anyone. Attorneys gave him the heebie-jeebies and the thought of having one after him for whatever reason gave him nightmares. So, anyone who came to work at Fabulous Cupcakes went legit.

"These noodles taste great," he said, ignoring the futile knocking from out front.

"We are closed!" Silvio waved his fork in the air, saying the words in a soft, singsong voice.

"Peanut spaghetti with tofu," Antonio said.

"Your English is getting better, you must be working hard at it," Daine said, noting how pleased Antonio looked at the compliment.

Daine was so hungry, he longed to upend the cardboard container and empty the contents into his mouth. Instead, he helped himself to the next dish, the sweet potato soup.

"Very good."

Silvio pointed his fork at the noodles. "You make cupcake like this?"

Daine looked at him. "How weird. I was just thinking that."

Silvio lifted his shoulders. "Is easy. Peanut and tofu."

Daine bit into the noodles again, trying to taste all the flavours.

Antonio imitated his mouth movements. Silvio closed his eyes.

"Spaghetti is good."

Daine agreed. "It is good."

"We have peanuts." Silvio's head tilted to the canisters lining the far wall.

Daine nodded. "And we have some tofu."

The three men looked at each other.

"Want to give it a go?" Daine asked.

Between the three of them, they raced around assembling ingredients. Antonio added a bit of spice to the mixture as Silvio cut butter into the cake flour on the mixing machine.

"Peanut butter. Just a little," Daine said.

Antonio opened a fresh jar and spooned some into the now-creamy mixture.

Silvio turned the machine off. They all tasted a little.

"Missing something." Silvio shook his head, disappointed.

"No…no. I think I have it."

Daine grabbed a huge knife and hand-smashed some red-skinned peanuts, leaving the skins on. He threw them in and Silvio revved up the mixer again.

They waited a minute, then tried again.

"Is good. Is make me wanna have sex," Silvio said.

"Me, too," Daine said. "Wait." He reached into the takeout container with the sautéed tofu and spooned some into the cake mix.

Once again, Silvio beat the mixture, which was now a creamy, tan colour.

"Hot diggity, I think we have it!" Daine said.

"Is so good, I wanna have sex...even with *you!*" Silvio exclaimed.

Antonio snorted and crossed himself, but all three men were pleased with their efforts.

Daine whipped up some icing and they waited for the cupcakes to bake. They'd made enough for eighteen of the special delicacies. Their industrial oven took twenty-two minutes and, in that time, Silvio dealt a round of cards for a hand of *conquian*, Spanish gin rummy. Daine was a terrible player because he hated to see anyone else lose, but on this evening, it was Silvio who played badly. He was excited about the new cupcakes and kept running over to the oven to check them out.

After the oven pinged and they removed the pan, allowing it to cool, none of the men could concentrate on the game. They put the cards back in their container and began cleaning up the kitchen. Daine grinned as Antonio and Silvio took turns touching the cake tops, checking for coolness. Neither man had been involved in the creation of a test batch before. They had trouble wrapping their heads around some of Daine and Cairo's crazier creations, but always admitted to their tastiness.

Finally, there was nothing left that needed to be cleaned. Daine iced the cupcakes, allowing the other men to top them with three different kinds of chopped peanuts, including a honey roasted one, and a sprinkle of tofu.

"This is it," Daine said.

"*Salud!*"

They clinked cupcakes, raised them to their lips and bit into them.

"Hot damn." Daine was ecstatic. *Wait until Cairo tastes these. She's always complaining she has too much to do around here.*

"Is dem good." Silvio rolled his eyes.

"Yes," Antonio said. He licked the frosting from his fingers. He was cute in a swarthy, helpless way.

Cut it out, Paradis. You're just lonely.

"We make tomorrow?" Antonio asked.

They all looked at each other.

"Yes!" they said in unison.

Daine took a couple of cakes home and gave the rest to Silvio and Antonio, who looked ecstatic. As Daine locked the store and walked outside, he caught a glimpse of movement across the road near the university. *Wow...how weird...coulda sworn that was Mr. Gorgeous.* He shook his head. Why would Mr. Gorgeous be here at this time of night hiding behind a tree? He unlocked the door to his '67 Chevy Impala. She was a classic car that didn't handle San Francisco's hills too well anymore, but she had sentimental value and Daine wasn't willing to give her up yet. He patted the dash. He shared digs with a couple of buddies in a pretty swanky apartment in nearby Nob Hill. He loved the area, even though it was one of the original seven hills in the city — one of San Francisco's forty-four. His Impala made it every time, but Daine prayed hard daily that she wouldn't get halfway up the steep incline and start rolling backward.

He passed the Tenderloin district, lowered the window and held his breath. The wind ruffled his hair and it felt nice against his skin as he pointed the car up California Street. The Impala whined all the way up the hill and he clenched his teeth on the last climb.

Bravo! He should buy a new car and he knew it, but it seemed an extravagance. He didn't spend much money on anything except the business. Maybe he should think about it a little more.

He turned into Mason Street and wondered if the guys would be home. His roommates, Ben and Steve, were a couple who provided and coordinated talent for live gay porn appearances for a major porn movie studio in the city. They provided go-go dancers, hot tub boys…you name it. They were rarely home these days, now that they'd developed a fan following themselves. They were very cool guys, but sometimes Daine felt hopelessly square around them. They had taken off for Palm Springs for its annual Hot n Dry party — the sober equivalent of the debauched White Party — the previous weekend and hadn't returned. He knew they were alive because they'd posted photos on their Facebook page and he'd received an alert since he'd been tagged on their page.

When he clicked the link, the tag said, "Yoo-hoo, Daine! Wish you were here."

Yeah, right.

He parked in the subterranean parking garage and took the elevator up to the seventh floor. None of them could have afforded the place on their own and he had to admit the view was stunning. He popped on lights and checked the mail. Bills. Of course. He could see the eastern portion of the city from the living room windows. The cable car museum glowed to his right. BART was still running, even at this hour. BART seemed to struggle with the hill, too.

Daine started undressing. He needed a shower and he needed rest. He was exhausted but somehow he wasn't sleepy. He had a weird, inexplicable feeling of doom and tried to tell himself not to be stupid.

He turned to his box of cupcakes. "It's just you and me now, cakes," he said and lifted the lid.

It took Phillip a long time to fall asleep. He had no idea why he'd gone back to the bakery, but he'd spied on Daine long enough to see him emerging from the place with a small box in his hands. Two other men had come out and he recognised them as the kitchen staff he'd seen earlier in the day. He wasn't sure if Daine had seen him and had jumped behind a tree just in time.

What he learned? Not much. Daine was a workaholic, which was not a crime. He apparently liked to work late, probably testing new recipes with his employees. Declan's initial research had shown there'd been some sort of a family disagreement, his parents had vanished, followed by his uncle a while later. Why had they left and not returned? How come Daine was estranged from all of them?

Phillip had already begun his report and made some headway in his background check. So far, everything he could dig up on the guy made him like him even more. Even his few bad reviews on Yelp complimented Daine's food. Their complaints seemed to target the sometimes slow service and the unpleasant personality of a pink-haired female shop assistant.

He'd go back to Fabulous Cupcakes in the morning and investigate further.

Oddly, he kept dreaming of snakes, cake boxes and tennis shoes, and when he woke up the next morning he was as tired as if he hadn't rested at all.

He did have breakfast to look forward to, though. A quick shower and shave later, he decided to go for the same casual clothes he'd worn yesterday. Attracting attention to his real profession by wearing a suit wouldn't be wise. He could always come back here and change before going into the office.

When he entered Fabulous Cupcakes just after eight a.m., the scent alone made him want to stay forever. Freshly brewed coffee mixed with cinnamon, vanilla and who knew what other mouth-watering substances. This was as close to paradise as he was likely to make it. Cinnamon roll cupcakes, dripping with icing, had been added to the display, as had a few cupcake varieties labelled 'breakfast'.

The scrambled egg and sausage cupcakes looked fascinating. These had samples and he couldn't resist trying them. Oh, they were good. They tasted like…well, sausage and eggs inside a spicy cupcake. He eyed the maple syrup and bacon cupcake. Dare he try it?

"Good morning." Daine's voice interrupted his reverie. "You came back."

"How could I not?" He grinned at the cute blush and almost lost himself in the greenest eyes he'd ever seen. "I loved the cherry pie cupcake yesterday and decided this might be a good place to come for breakfast as well."

"I'm glad you liked it." Daine smiled. "Do you work near here? We can deliver breakfast to you if you want to give us a standing order."

"I teach law at the university." Well, he did. The thought of having Daine deliver breakfast made his pants feel slightly tight. He'd rather have him in his bed, but serving him a meal in bed was a good start.

"That's definitely within our range. I hope you'll give it some thought." Daine pointed at the breakfast display.

"As you can see, the breakfast choices are quite creative, if you're willing to experiment. But we serve a more traditional hot breakfast as well, even though it's very basic."

"I'd like to combine the two." *Adding a side of Daine, if possible.* "I'll take the basic hot breakfast, please." He scanned the day's menu. "I'll have an omelette and toast."

Daine nodded.

"Coffee, of course, and then I'll try the cornflake and raspberry cupcake." He paid for his food and took a seat in the corner, watching Daine deal with other customers. His breakfast was delicious, but he stayed once he was done eating. He was here to gather information, after all.

Daine was unfailingly friendly to all his customers, but, even so, the number of people that streamed into the store and left with big bags of food was amazing. Two employees helped Daine behind the counter and two more were trying to keep up with the orders from the eat-in area.

A girl with giddy pink hair drifted in at ten. This had to be the woman mentioned in a couple of online reviews.

"Hey, Cairo." Daine seemed pleased to see her.

"I've been experimenting with new icing flavours," she said, in a tone suggesting she'd discovered a cure for the common cold.

The bakery had filled quickly after Phillip had arrived and there wasn't a free chair in sight for the next hour. He watched Cairo take her time putting things away, checking her hair, tasting samples, making calls. She took a couple of breakfast cheques from people waiting and rang them up. Everybody else ran rings around her. She was a piece of work.

Daine didn't show any hostility, though. Maybe he was used to it. If she was the creator of these...er...fabulous cupcakes, maybe that was why.

Phillip knew he couldn't keep hogging a table without ordering something else so he beckoned Daine over, asking for a coffee refill.

"And what is the cupcake flavour of the day?"

"We have a couple, but today we're trying out a new one I created last night after the store closed. My two bakers and I ate some Thai food and—"

"How funny, I had Thai food last night, too."

Daine smiled. "I wanted pizza, but I'm so happy the guys ignored me and went all the way into Union Square to get food from The King of Thai."

Phillip stared at him. What were the chances?

"We got the peanut and tofu spaghetti and—"

"That's my favourite dish," Phillip said.

Daine beamed. "Really? Then you must try the cupcake. On the house, since I'd value your opinion."

Still in shock over their shared tastes in food, Phillip sat with the news, rolling the ideas around in his brain.

When Daine brought the cupcake to him on a small plate, he was surprised to see the two bakers flanking him.

"We make," one of them said, pointing from himself to the other guy. The man had a mouth full of gold teeth. Phillip hoped he didn't walk around after dark with his mouth open. He'd be a sitting duck.

He dutifully bit into the cupcake and almost swooned.

"Oh, my God. It's delicious." He glanced up to see three sets of eyes watching his every facial expression. "It's exactly how the dish tastes. It's really good! How'd you do that?"

The three men were too busy high-fiving each other to respond. Phillip noticed the venomous look on Cairo's face. As quickly as the expression arrived, however, that particular train soon left the station.

A few seconds later, a group of tiny Girl Scout Brownies entered the store with a stern-looking woman. The girls were giggly and cute. Phillip found himself utterly entranced by them. They were so sweet. They presented

Daine with a gigantic poster they'd made by hand, thanking Fabulous Cupcakes for all the cake donations the bakery had made to their annual Girl Scout picnic.

"Thank you, ladies," he said, hugging them all. He told the girls to each pick out a cupcake and began to pin the poster on the wall. He struggled with the pins, so Phillip helped. Their hands met in the middle and Daine seemed to be breathing as hard as he was at the touch.

Daine glanced at Phillip and broke eye contact first.

"I'll finish this, you take care of the girls," Phillip said.

He studied the photographs in the poster. Daine had donated dozens of cakes to the girls for the third year in a row. As far as Phillip could tell, this was a hard-working guy with a strong sense of team-playing, judging by the way he credited the bakers for helping him create the new cupcake. And he was a man with a strong sense of community spirit. He clearly worked hard. And damn it, he was handsome. If he were a cupcake he'd be a cross between a Creamsicle and a Hot Tamales. Phillip could almost taste the spicy cinnamon candy in his mouth just thinking about it.

He turned to find Cairo giving him an appraising glance. He felt a shiver go through him. She was an oddball, that one.

He finished his coffee at the bar running along one side of the room. He'd lost his table putting up the poster. Having tasted the food here, he could see why people kept coming back. Was it something in the cupcakes themselves?

This would require more research, possibly a different approach. There was only so much information he could get by sitting around in the store and watching the goings on. Only Daine had the real answers, so he'd need to find a way to talk to him, ask him more detailed questions.

That wasn't going to happen while the store was open. He'd thought the traffic would die down, but it hadn't slowed much by ten-thirty, so he could forget that idea. The lunch rush would start soon, and then he'd never get Daine on his own.

What he needed was a new strategy.

"You lost your table?" Suddenly Daine stood next to him, looking mortified.

"Yeah."

"I'm sorry."

"Hey, don't apologise. I like watching people come in and enjoy the food." There, that wasn't too far from the truth.

"You're welcome to stay as long as you want." Daine hesitated. "You don't have a class to teach this morning?"

"No, nothing today at all, actually." He pointed at the stool beside him. "Do you have time to join me for a moment?"

Daine looked around the store and nodded. It seemed only marginally less hectic than a little while ago to Phillip, but Daine surely knew what he was doing. He sat next to Phillip and they chatted about food for a while. Phillip really enjoyed talking to Daine. When there was a short pause in their conversation, it was time to get up his courage.

"I was wondering if you'd like to come see a movie with me tonight. Take a break from it all. Sounds to me like you need it." He held his breath as emotions flitted across Daine's expressive face.

Surprise was quickly followed with pleasure and Daine nodded.

"That's a yes, huh?" He was delighted. Until he remembered that he was supposed to spy on the man, find out his secrets.

Shit.

* * * *

Daine was still in shock when he closed up the shop at the end of the day. It had been another very busy one. He didn't know what had made him so successful all of a sudden two years ago, but he wasn't going to complain.

He hadn't been asked on a date in a very long time. He hadn't been looking for anything either. The store had always taken priority. His ambition, combined with his uncle's constant needling — about how he wasn't going to make it because he was a failure — had made sure of that.

Now that his shop was one of the most successful cupcake stores in San Francisco, if not *the* most successful, there should be some time to relax. He flinched when he remembered next week's Annual Cupcake Competition. It would decide who made the best and most creative cupcakes. A separate category took into account participants' business results and the end result was the title of "Best Cupcakes in San Francisco", which came with a free consultation about expanding the winner's franchise.

The last two years' winners were now multimillionaires.

He wasn't as bothered about the money, although he wouldn't turn it down. No, what he was really interested in was some sort of recognition that would make his uncle shut up.

He could have driven back to Nob Hill, but there was a tiny apartment upstairs he used as a stockroom, test kitchen and crash pad. Tonight was one of the times he was tired enough to make use of it.

Daine slowly walked up the stairs to the apartment. His parents had insisted he finish college first, and he had respected their wishes, but this had always been his passion. People and food. Too bad things were so strained between him and his parents now. He still didn't quite understand it. They had moved to Venezuela...three years it had been since their last contact. It surprised him. He still, in his heart of hearts, expected to pick up the phone one day and hear his mom's voice.

What he needed was a shower and a change of clothes before his first date in years. Spending two hours in the dark, sitting next to Mr. Gorgeous, um, Phillip sounded like heaven. Daine should really stop referring to him as Mr. Gorgeous before he started calling Phillip that to his face.

All he needed to do now was stay awake until Phillip came to pick him up. Just thinking about the man, maybe holding hands, touching him, had him going hard. He'd better make it a cold shower then. That would also help dampen his arousal.

An hour later he was combing his hair, trying to decide whether to leave it down or pull it back into a ponytail, when the doorbell rang. He checked his watch. His date was two minutes early. He grinned as he opened the door.

"Hi." Phillip looked almost as nervous as Daine felt. He scanned Daine from top to bottom and grinned.

"Hi, yourself. You want to come in for a minute?" Daine stepped aside to let him in. Phillip didn't look half bad in the tightest jeans known to man and a dark green T-shirt. There went the benefit of his cold shower. His jeans were suddenly way tighter than they'd been before Phillip arrived. "I'll be quick."

Almost running for cover, he made his way back to the bathroom, closed the door and leaned against it, breathing heavily. How was he going to get through several hours next to Phillip without exploding?

When he'd finally got himself under some sort of control again, he tied back his hair, checked himself in the mirror and made his way back into the living room. Phillip got up from the sofa and walked towards him, squinting.

"I think I liked you better before you ran off." Phillip took his hand and pulled him up against his body.

"Y-you did?" Daine was having trouble breathing again. The hard muscles of the other man pressed against him from knee to chest were not helping.

"Yeah." Phillip moved slowly, as if to give him time to push away. "I kinda liked you with your hair loose."

"Oh." Daine was certain he sounded like an idiot, but the scent of Phillip's cologne, his arm around his middle and the smouldering look in his eyes were too distracting.

"May I?" Phillip reached behind his head, resting his fingers on the rubber band he'd used.

He nodded. He'd let Phillip do anything he wanted as long as he kept him in his arms. Phillip very slowly and carefully removed the rubber band, dropping it into his pocket. Phillip lifted his hand again, burying it in Daine's hair, angling his head upwards.

"I've been wanting to touch your hair. I knew it would feel like this."

Oh, man. I might come right now. Yes! Please, kiss me.

As if Phillip had read Daine's mind, he bent his head and kissed him. Daine pulled back immediately as if to check if everything was okay. It was more than okay. It was wonderful. His smile must have given him away because Phillip smiled back and brushed his lips across Daine's a few times before placing little kisses along his mouth and licking the corner.

God, that feels good. He opened on a sigh and let his own tongue come out to play. Their careful touches slowly morphed into a heated exchange of small kisses, licks and caresses that made Daine go rock-hard in his tight jeans. Phillip used the arm he'd put around his middle to pull him closer and licked inside Daine's mouth. The kiss went on and on, low sighs accompanying their harsh breathing. It was so hot, Daine wanted to start grinding his hips, looking for friction. Shit, he was almost ready to come.

It wouldn't have taken much more and he would have embarrassed himself. But Phillip pulled back just before it was too late. His pupils were dilated with lust and his breathing was faster than usual.

"We need to leave if we don't want to miss the show." Phillip didn't look like he'd be too bothered.

"I've been looking forward to it." Maybe he should just give in?

Phillip took Daine's hand, bringing it to his lips. "We can always continue this later, right?"

Chapter Three

There was no later. The two men kissed and dry-humped like teens.

"I don't know what's come over me," Phillip murmured, looking for a soft spot to lay down the hard man between his legs.

"Is that your bed?" His gaze rested on an Asian daybed tucked beneath the window, fascinated.

"Yeah. This is where I come to sleep when I'm tired." Daine sounded winded.

"Are you tired now?" Phillip asked. "Would you like to lie down?"

"Oh, yeah. I'm exhausted. I'd *love* to lie down."

"Good…good. I'm tired too."

He pushed Daine to the bed, which was surprisingly comfortable. He lay on top of Daine, their gazes colliding. *Oh, man, I can feel his hard cock against mine.*

Daine's grin was contagious. Boyish and lust-filled at the same time.

Phillip began to rub his cock against Daine's rigid shaft. Even fully-clothed, this was an erotic high for him. Daine was soft, hard, sweet, sexy and hot, hot, hot.

Their kisses deepened.

"The movie's supposed to be crap anyway," Daine said when he caught his breath.

"We hadn't picked one yet. But yeah…it would be crap." He gasped when Daine's pelvis jutted harder against him. Phillip didn't think he could take much more intense friction like this.

"Oh, man," Daine whispered. Phillip sensed the other man's orgasm and didn't skip a beat. Keeping the same, measured pace, he watched Daine's face as it registered the looming moment of impact. Damn. Phillip wanted it to be so good for Daine, but now he was coming, too. With fistfuls of Daine's blond hair in his hands, his body responded to the sensations of Daine's legs tightening around him, his cries inflaming Phillip even more.

They both came hard, still glued to one another.

Wow.

"That beats any movie," Daine finally said.

"Even gay porn," Phillip said.

They both laughed and kissed. Phillip felt close to the guy, finding it endearing when Daine's cheeks pinked and he looked away, becoming bashful.

"It's been a long time for me," he said.

"Me, too." Phillip kissed him, raising himself on an elbow. "I'd like to see what got me all hot and bothered." He reached for Daine's zipper.

His phone beeping distracted him.

"Damn." He did not need this gadget interrupting him.

"Anything wrong?"

"My assistant."

"Maybe you should take the call?"

"It can wait. He'll leave a message."

Phillip unzipped Daine's jeans and finally got a look at the half-hard cock wedged uncomfortably in his tight, black boxer briefs. It was huge. Phillip could hardly contain his pleasure at the sight of it. He licked his lips, his tongue touching the cock head he held reverently in his fingertips.

His phone kept ringing.

Daine touched his back. "Maybe you should answer."

"Yeah. Maybe I should."

Phillip leant back, checking the call. Declan had left text messages and voice mail. He had to get back to the office. He looked at the beautiful man on the bed who tried so hard not to look disappointed.

"I'll make this up to you, I promise."

Daine smiled. "Kiss me when you say that."

* * * *

Phillip was embarrassed when Declan grilled him as soon as he'd reached the office. Eleven p.m. What the hell was the big emergency?

"You humped him? What are you? Sixteen?" Declan's eyebrows had crept up his forehead far enough to be in danger of disappearing under his hairline.

"Keep your voice down." Phillip was pissed off. The situation with Daine was definitely heating up. And now he'd gone and told Declan about it. What the hell was wrong with him? He'd never become involved with a suspect before. He'd got to know plenty of them, using all the wiles the Superpower Court system deemed appropriate, but Daine was like cupcakes. Easy to look at. Hard to resist.

"Honey, your investigation just took a sharp turn onto What the Fuck Boulevard." Declan's hostile tone jerked him away from his reverie.

Phillip stared at him. "Honey? Did you just call me honey?"

What the hell had got into Declan lately? Being with Daine had been the sweetest thing to happen to Phillip for a long time. Rolling around on Daine's daybed like teenagers had turned out to be a superb date. Dry humping was underrated, in Phillip's opinion. He was starting to develop feelings for Daine that took What the Fuck Boulevard straight into Holy Shit I'm Screwed Cul-de-Sac. Not that he announced this aloud. He already felt bad for having blurted news of his romantic state when he barged into the office, but really, Declan was getting outlandish in his behaviour.

He felt a protectiveness towards Daine that he just couldn't explain. There was a tragedy to Daine's life he couldn't quite grasp, but it was there.

"Mr. Arden would like to see you now," Declan said. His eyebrows were back down where they belonged, but he kept clicking the end of his pen in an aggravating way. Phillip took it out of Declan's fingers and put it on the desk with a clack.

"Thanks. *Honey*." Phillip threw the word back at him, pleased to see that the other man looked embarrassed.

He knocked and entered Mr. Arden's office. Mr. Arden looked as grumpy as Phillip felt.

"How is your investigation coming along?"

"Fine," Phillip said, feeling nervous and uncomfortable in his sticky underpants and jeans. He took a seat and hoped that Mr. Arden wasn't going to make what had started out as a pleasant evening into a miserable one.

"Do we have enough to sue him?"

"Sue him?" Phillip didn't think he could be hearing right. "Not at all. I mean, I've spent two days on the case and, so far, this guy seems to be legitimate. I don't see any abuse of superpowers here at all."

Mr. Arden's expression was bleak.

"Sir," Phillip finished lamely.

"Tell me what you have so far." Mr. Arden steepled his fingers together and leant back in his chair.

"He works long days. He has some staff problems. He has a kitchen full of immigrants but I checked their records and all their paperwork is in order. He bakes from scratch. He doesn't seem to...conjure anything out of thin air. If you'll forgive me, sir, I think this is a wild goose chase."

"I'll decide when the goose gets caught and cooked, Mr. Sedgwick."

"But, sir, like I said, I just see a man who's working hard doing very well. I have no evidence—yet—of abuse of power."

"Humph."

Mr. Arden pressed a button on his tiny, black remote control. It was a lethal piece of machinery. It doubled as a judge's gavel, a weapon and—right now—a portal key.

"Tell it to the judge, Mr. Sedgwick."

Phillip felt a rush of cool air and he was rising. He'd been picked out for this gig years ago, had won his share of trials, yet he still trembled at the knees when he entered the Superpower Courtroom. He could hear voices. A man and a woman.

The chill made him feel it must have been a Water-Power trial but, as he and Mr. Arden took the winding stairs that spilled out to the courtyard, Phillip saw people waiting their turn and felt their heat. He was wrong. It was a Fire-Power trial.

Judge Sexby presided over the Court of Revelation. He was a fire-breathing hellion, literally, but Phillip had interned under the elderly justice and respected him. Judge Sexby's speciality was abuse of power, and he could be eloquent on the subject. Phillip hovered in one of the many arched openings to the courtroom. There were no doors in the Fire Court. Things tended to get overheated at the best of times between complainants, let alone when Judge Sexby got irate.

Two men stood on one side, and a woman stood at the opposite side of the court. Phillip focussed on the men. He recognised the good-looking one as movie star Jake Merit. Judge Sexby, he of the silver-haired, blue-eyed, wrinkle-free countenance, sat rigid in his chair, his bailiff staring at the actor in disbelief.

Judge Sexby held up his hand.

"Come now, Mr. Merit, you expect me to believe that, having given you a chance after you were arrested on drunk driving charges in Santa Monica, California, given the opportunity to turn your life around, you haven't figured out how to do it?"

"I have no moral compass, Your Honour." The actor grinned. Some of the jurors tittered. Phillip picked out the twin seers of the town of Pryor. They always liked handsome men. One of them winked at Phillip. He winked back, careful that Judge Sexby wasn't watching him.

"That's true." Judge Sexby silenced the tittering in the court with a raised hand. "I'm afraid you've exhausted all your appeals and I find I am out of time…not to mention patience, so here is my sentence. You are hereby stripped of your supernatural powers and all your worldly possessions. You may not appear in any major motion pictures, nor anything that requires merchandising of your likeness—"

"But, Your Honour!"

Judge Sexby kept talking. "You may not win another Academy Award, Emmy Award...or..." Judge Sexby stared hard at the horrified actor, "People's Choice Award. You may not appear on the cover of magazines or newspapers and you will refrain from bedding women who are likely to have tabloid paparazzi following you."

"But, Your *Honour!*"

"You may appear only on reality shows that can help fray the costs of your spousal and child support cases. May I suggest you start with *Celebrity Rehab* where you can tell your fans all about the randomness of fortune?"

He banged his gavel.

"I'd rather die, Your Honour."

"That can be arranged, Mr. Merit."

Merit's attorney obviously realised Judge Sexby was getting ready to huff, puff and blow the actor down and tugged him away.

"You wanted to see me, Mr. Arden?" Judge Sexby waved Mr. Arden and Phillip into the court.

Man, it was hot. Phillip felt his temperature soar in an unpleasant way. He spotted some of the toughest jurors in the system taking up the twelve seats. Two of them were experienced, venerated members of the Fire Court. He recognised the Mage of Berwick, a man who reputedly could shape-shift into animals and useful household objects. There was the fire-king of Hesbia. He watched Phillip, who nodded at him. The fire-king was a hot dude, but inclined to become nuts if you dumped him. Or so Phillip had been told.

He caught the gaze of Merit's prosecuting counsel, one of the women from Phillip's law firm. She gave him a curt nod. She didn't look happy about having her big victory swamped by an unscheduled court appearance by their boss.

She walked away quickly as Mr. Arden took her place on the prosecution's side of the room.

"Your Honour, thank you for allowing me to disrupt your busy schedule."

"Don't brown-nose me, Arden. Spit it out. We're busy people...so many lives to ruin...so little time."

"Your Honour, I am requesting permission to hasten the trial date of Superpowers versus Paradis." Mr. Arden stared straight ahead.

"Why? As far as I know, Mr. Sedgwick was given a week to come up with proof that Daine Paradis, owner of Fabulous Cupcakes, is abusing his powers. Are there any reasons why he would require less than the allotted time?" Judge Sexby frowned.

"Your Honour," Phillip said, rushing to move to opposing counsel position. "On the contrary. I was handed this case two days ago and I have made a great start into my preparation, but I hardly think it's fair to deny me the rest of the week when—"

"Have you found any proof of abuse?" Judge Sexby asked Phillip.

"No, Your Honour."

"Mr. Sedgwick, I'll see you in chambers."

Judge Sexby had taken Mr. Arden by surprise. That much was evident. His boss looked stunned as Phillip rushed by him and followed the judge into his chambers. He'd never been asked back there in all his years of superpower trials. Phillip glanced around, trying to take it all in. Finally his gaze returned to the judge and, as had recently become his habit, flew to the justice's feet. Snakeskin boots. They were creepy, since they seemed to be a pair of snakes, with glass eyes at the toes, in place of real ones. They were slitty eyes, not round. According to Billy the Exterminator that meant the snakes had been venomous. *Holy shit...this is one tough hombre. I didn't need to see his boots to know that, but still...*

"I killed the snakes myself. They were sent to me...courtesy of a convicted felon. A pair of Inland Taipans. World's deadliest snakes. They look good on me, don't you think?"

"Yes, sir, I do."

"Humph." Judge Sexby took a seat, indicating that Phillip should sit on the other side of his desk. The judge brought out a small black portable digital organiser and studied it.

"I see that you have got...quite close to your suspect. You don't think this will compromise your case against him?"

"No, sir, I don't."

"Well, I've always said, gay men have no real, deep feelings. It's all a big bunch of hooey." Judge Sexby waved a hand in the air as if to brush away an unpleasant thought.

Steady on. That's not true.

"So, I'll allow you the five remaining days, and I look forward to seeing you in court, Mr. Sedgwick. Is there anything else?" Judge Sexby looked up with eyebrows raised.

"No, sir." Phillip was careful to shutter his feelings and thoughts from the judge. It infuriated him that gay people were discriminated against even by higher powers.

He felt Mr. Arden's tap on his shoulder and they were back in the office again. If Phillip hadn't known any better, he could have sworn the whole incident had been a figment of his imagination, but he knew it hadn't been.

"Sorry," Mr. Arden said, looking like he actually was. "Declan persuaded me that you were becoming over-involved with Daine Paradis. You are my best investigator. I should have trusted you."

"Yes, you should have."

"Declan lists several grievances against Paradis…including the fact that the man doesn't speak to his parents."

"If we're going to judge people based on family dynamics, the whole world will wind up on trial," Phillip pointed out.

"True." Mr. Arden studied him a moment. "You understand the significance though, Mr. Sedgwick."

Phillip considered the implication. "You mean that Daine's father was once a respected judge in the Fire Court but fell from grace?" Before Mr. Arden could respond, Phillip stood. "I'll find out what I can. Maybe Daine really has no clue. I'm not just saying this, but based on what I've seen so far, I'm inclined to believe he doesn't even know that he has powers of any kind."

Mr. Arden nodded.

"May I ask why this case has become so hot all of a sudden?"

Mr. Arden didn't respond to the question.

"Carry on, Mr. Sedgwick. I'll talk to Declan myself."

"Please do that," Phillip said. He walked straight past Declan's desk and kept his gaze away from the man. He was so angry he couldn't speak. What was going on with Declan? Was it time for a new assistant?

He hated to think about the hassle involved with going through that formality, not to mention training a new assistant. He checked the time. Just past midnight. He wanted to see Daine. Badly.

Phillip called him from the confines of his car. Daine answered his phone on the second ring.

"Hey, I was just thinking about you."

Good. That means he's still awake.

"You got room for me in that sexy bed of yours? I do believe we have some unfinished business." Phillip needed a distraction from all this stress.

"Sure I do. Get your ass over here. I just watched that actor Jake Merit get arrested at Malibu Pier. He used all kinds of F bombs...he was totally stoned and drunk. He blamed black people, white people, gay people and women. He's ranting on TV now about the abuse of power." Daine chuckled.

Wow, that was fast. "Can I help you forget all your troubles...and his?"

Daine laughed. "Abso-fucking-lutely. I'm naked. I'm in bed. And I want you."

* * * *

Phillip was pleased to see that Daine was a man of his words. Well, almost. He was naked, but he'd had to leave the sexy Asian daybed upstairs to let Phillip in. He followed Daine's hot ass into the apartment, wondering where he put all those cupcakes.

"Something smells good," Phillip said, sniffing appreciatively as they entered the apartment. "Buttered popcorn!"

"Almost."

"*Almost?*"

Daine closed the door behind them. "Buttered popcorn cupcakes."

Phillip almost swooned. "Really?"

Daine walked to the small kitchen and Phillip followed. A dozen beautifully iced cupcakes lay on a plate.

"Wow...they look ready to be photographed." Phillip took in the buttery-yellow frosting, the glazed popcorn topping and, below these artful creations, a serving platter of the same colour.

"You're expecting company?"

"Nope. I rarely crave cupcakes...you came along and bingo. Sexual frustration means I crave comfort food." He shrugged. "The baking also helps me deal with my nervous energy."

Phillip turned and looked at him, wide-eyed.

"Can I...may I touch one?"

"I wish you would. I'm in danger of eating most of them otherwise." Daine grinned.

Phillip reached out and swiped some frosting, sucking it from his fingertip. He could feel his toes curling in his shoes. "Oh wow, this just does it for the kid in me."

"What about the adult?" Daine stepped forward, nuzzling Phillip, his hand going straight to Phillip's pants.

"Oh...big Phillip—" Daine's fingers had found Phillip's cock and began massaging the head, "little Phillip...all the Phillips like it. A lot."

Daine ran a finger through the icing, feeding some to Phillip, who sucked the tip suggestively.

"Beneath that geeky exterior beats the heart of a very bad boy," Daine said, unzipping Phillip's fly.

"Geeky?" Phillip was pretty sure he should be offended but he wasn't. Apparently Daine liked geeky. Oh... He had bent down and was focussed on sucking Phillip's cock. Phillip silently urged him, *yes, yes, yes!*

"When I was a kid, I thought I could fly," he said, suddenly. Daine held Phillip's cock in his hand, sliding his fingers up and down the shaft.

He straightened, using his free hand to slip more icing into Phillip's mouth. Phillip sucked the sweet cream, relishing the flavour burst of salty popcorn.

"How did you do that?" he murmured. "The taste is incredible."

"And did you fly?"

Actually, yes. That's when I knew I was a total weirdo.

"No," he said, hating to lie, but he had to.

"But you tried?"

"Of course."

"Hmmm…well, I'm glad you survived."

"Me, too." Phillip sucked in a breath. Daine's fingers worked on his shaft and his balls now. He wanted the man to suck him again. He wanted to come in his mouth.

"I want you to take off all your clothes and sit in the leather chair by the bed for me," Daine said.

Phillip raced into the other room and did as he was told. He was waiting in the chair, his legs half-open when Daine came in, holding a cupcake in the palm of his hands.

"This, my friend, is what is known as having your cupcake, and eating it, too."

Daine handed the cake to him, pulled his legs wide open, kneeling between them. He began sucking on Phillip's balls as he placed Phillip's feet on the chair. He took his mouth away.

"Scoot to the edge, baby."

Phillip became lost in the sensations, yearning to eat his cake. He licked the frosting as Daine's tongue swirled around the tender skin of his inner thighs. First the left, then the right, dipping down to his balls. He almost screamed for cock-to-mouth contact and got it before he could utter a sound.

Daine sucked on his cock, his finger reaching up and dipping into the icing of the cupcake. Phillip watched as Daine's finger plunged all the way into the cake and came out again, covered in cream.

He held it to Phillip's mouth. Phillip sucked, matching the intensity of Daine's mouth and came so hard it surprised them both.

"Oh, man," he said, looking down, dazed as Daine held his still-erupting cock tightly at the base.

They jumped into bed and ate cake and icing together. Phillip was anxious to fuck the man who'd brought him such bliss, but Daine kissed him and said, "Sorry, babe, I'm a baker. I gotta go bake."

Phillip checked the time. Four a.m.

"But you've had no sleep."

Daine shrugged. "I had fun. I hope you did, too."

"I...I..." Phillip was overcome with a mixture of emotions. He hadn't reciprocated and he wanted to. He knew how hard Daine worked. He also knew in that moment that Daine was not successful because of any misuse of superpowers. He worked damned hard. If only he knew how powerful he was, his life would be much easier...or would it?

He knew in his heart he could not prosecute this man. He cared about him too much. He would do everything in his power to defend him.

"Get some sleep, I'll bring you some breakfast," Daine said, slipping on fresh clothes.

"I only want you," Phillip said, and promptly fell asleep.

* * * *

Phillip arrived on campus in clothes borrowed from Daine, carrying a huge turkey and watercress sandwich, a scoop of home-made apple coleslaw, half a dozen assorted cupcakes and a Thermos full of hot coffee. He also had a hot date with Daine planned for later that night.

"Nice shirt," one of the female lecturers said, fingering the collar. "What's that smell?" She sniffed. "Oh, God...you've been to Fabulous Cupcakes!"

"No, I haven't," he lied and scuttled away.

"Yes, you have!" she shrieked, like he was a thief in the night. "I know that smell anywhere. It's mango, chilli, lime and salt!"

He hid his bounty in his staff locker he never used, once he remembered the combination. He locked it, making sure nobody had seen him opening it. He had to hide his mango stash. Daine had brought him breakfast in bed. Phillip had wanted to have a little taste of Paradis...but he'd had to settle for the day's speciality, a mango cupcake. He'd flipped out, downing three before he left the apartment above the bakery.

Phillip ran to his class and found the kids staring at him expectantly. Aw, nuts. He'd had such a great day two days before. Now he was going to lose them again.

"Abuse of power," he said, standing before the class. "Anyone know what that means?"

The kids still seemed bright-eyed. A few hands shot up and people tossed out responses. The girl who'd been reading the shoe book stared at him, hard.

"I know you have something to say," he said. "What is it?"

"Well...the book I've been reading..."

God help me...not the damned shoe book again...

"*The History of the Rod* by William A. Cooper talks about how the abuse of power has always been punished, even in ancient Egypt." She held up a book. Man, this girl was spooky. She had the most unusual tastes of any young woman he'd met.

His astonishment must have been mistaken for fascination because she began to rant about the history of whipping and flagellation.

"Did you know whipping was once used for medical purposes?"

A titter went around the room.

The student nodded, warming to her macabre theme. "Convent nuns were whipped—and I bet they enjoyed it, too. Queens were flogged, but I'm guessing with them, not so much."

Some of the students were laughing outright now.

"The breast and penis are two favourite parts of the body for whipping—"

"Your point being?" Phillip asked, cringing at the thought of somebody flogging his private parts.

"Well, people abuse power because they want to be beaten," she said, nodding knowingly. "It's a very strong part of erotic romanticism."

What?

Phillip finally brought the class back under control to a more pertinent area, the abuse of power in the judicial system.

As soon as class ended, he put a call through to Daine.

"How do you feel about flagellation?" he asked.

There was a significant pause.

"Why are you asking me this?" Daine asked. Phillip could hear the sounds of voices and realised his lover was having a tough day.

"One of my students claims it's erotic and romantic."

Daine finally laughed. "Not to me, babe. I'm a cake guy. Listen, I hate to cut you off, but I gotta run. I'm having the day from hell here. The health department just showed up. This crazy woman came in two days ago and bought a single lemon bar cupcake and is now claiming food poisoning. I feel I'm being railroaded. Something weird is going on here."

Phillip opened his mouth to speak, but sighed instead.

"Gotta run," Daine said again. "A fight's broken out in the bakery because they won't let me serve the customers until the inspection is over."

Phillip heard a tremendous crash, the sound of someone screaming.

Then the line went dead.

* * * *

Daine put his phone away, covered his face with his hands and moaned quietly as he got up, ready to jump back into the fray to try and calm some nerves. Could this day get any worse? As soon as he'd asked the question, he knew it most probably would, just because he'd dared to think about it.

Last night with Phillip had been very special. He'd felt a connection with the professor, one that seemed to promise more than a quick tumble between the sheets. He was starting to hope he might have found someone who could become a real partner.

Phillip had even returned to him after their date had been so rudely interrupted by his assistant. What kind of college professor had to run into the office after eight p.m. anyway? There couldn't possibly be an emergency that urgent so late at night. God, what if something fishy was going on with Phillip as well?

It was hard enough dealing with all the goings-on at the bakery. He opened the door of his tiny office at the back, the noise immediately attacking his ears. To his left he could see a few impatient customers standing outside, waiting to be let in despite the sign on the door that said *temporarily closed.*

His assistant, Cairo, had taken a seat at one of the little tables and was reading a magazine. Why was she so relaxed? One of the health inspectors was still checking the counters. From the looks of it she was almost done, making copious notes on some form as she went.

The second inspector had entered the kitchen area of the bakery just as Daine's phone rang. The man had insisted that Antonio and Silvio accompany him into the kitchen in case he had any questions. Daine hadn't wanted to leave them to their own devices, but he'd wanted to take Phillip's call in private.

Before he had time to think about it, another crash from the bakery reminded him he'd better get over there.

"I-I'm sorry." Antonio was pale, standing next to the rack of baking trays with shaking hands. One of the trays was on the floor, another one already in the washing up area.

"Just don't get in my way again." The grumpy inspector with the horn-rimmed glasses was busy checking the ovens.

When he was done, he made notes before turning to the rest of the kitchen. Not a single surface was safe from him, nor were the insides of cupboards or the floor and all the corners. The man was frowning as if there were major issues, but Daine knew there was nothing to worry about. He kept everything squeaky clean.

The woman who'd bought the lemon cupcake had been very particular about her dietary requirements—being a vegan and all—then had gone on to eat a distinctly non-vegan sample of the cupcakes with the blue and green bubblegum icing. That was most likely what had caused her upset stomach.

Of course, the health inspectors hadn't been interested in his explanation and had insisted on going ahead with the full procedure. It looked a lot like some sort of sabotage to him. Who was doing this — and why?

It wasn't just the loss of business. He kept thinking about the upcoming Annual Cupcake Competition. He'd wanted to make a start on working on recipe ideas today, but, with all this hoopla, he'd need the rest of the day just to sort out the mess and backlog from this morning.

"Do you think we'll be okay?" Antonio stood next to him as the health inspector finally left the kitchen and joined his colleague at another one of the small tables.

"We should be." Daine rubbed his temples, trying to forestall the headache he knew was coming. "You know how careful we are about keeping everything clean. The equipment is up to standard, so is the building. I can't imagine anything other than the stupidity of eating something she shouldn't have causing that customer's digestive issues."

"Mr. Paradis?" The grumpy inspector looked up from his notes. "If you would like to come over here, please?"

"Certainly." Daine walked over and took a seat.

"As you know, we did this inspection to follow up on a customer complaint about food poisoning." The grumpy man's frown deepened. "That is a very serious allegation and we have followed the procedures to the letter."

Was the man trying to scare him with that statement? Daine wasn't about to admit how nervous he was, so he just nodded.

"We have examined everything from the raw materials storage, through the manufacturing area, the finished goods room, sales area, customer area and access to the premises." The man checked his list. "We have also examined the health and safety instructions for the staff."

Daine knew all that. He was about to kick the official to make sure the man managed to say what he obviously found very difficult.

"We have found nothing at fault." The inspector grimaced, as if he was in pain.

"Thank you." Even though he hadn't really doubted everything was fine, the relief was still considerable. "Are we free to open the store, then?"

"Yes. For now." The inspector ground out the words as he tore a pink sheet off his clipboard and handed it to Daine. "This is your temporary report, showing that you are being put on probation. Don't lose it. If there is no further offence within the next month, you will be sent the final assessment and certificate."

Daine's jaw dropped. Probationary clearance? That didn't even exist. What the hell was going on here?

Chapter Four

"Okay, guys, I'm gonna open the doors. Get ready, everyone outside looks ravenous. No wonder, it's almost ten." Daine had let the inspectors out the back exit so they wouldn't need to face the impatient crowd of waiting customers. He wasn't keen on everyone seeing he'd had the city's least welcome officials in his shop, either.

"Cairo, could you please take your spot behind the counter? I'm going to need all the help I can get if we want to make it today."

"Sure." Cairo got up with slow, lazy movements that made him crazy. Was she trying to provoke him into yelling at her? What was wrong with the woman? He shook his head. He needed to talk to her at some point soon. She was a great icing designer, but her attitude pissed him off.

"Sorry for the delay." Daine took a step back as a wave of eager men and women almost ran him over to make it into the store. There was some jostling before a more or less orderly line formed. Jeez, people were acting as if there was a famine out there.

That was his last conscious thought for a few hours. He barely kept up with demand—lunch hour starting almost as soon as the first wave of late breakfasters and morning snack seekers had been served to their satisfaction. Tray after tray of cupcakes was brought out, Silvio and Antonio looking as harried as he felt by the early afternoon.

It was nice to be successful, but this was ridiculous. He'd have to hire someone to help him with sales or he'd never find the time to finish his preparations for the upcoming competition. He only had a few days left as it was, and he hadn't even started finalising the recipes he'd use. Maybe one of Phillip's students was interested in a part-time job? At least they'd be able to speak English…he assumed.

"Are you okay?" Phillip's voice hit him totally unexpectedly as he was bending down to pick up some coins he'd carelessly dropped.

"Shit." His hands were shaking as he put the small change into the register where it belonged. His stomach growled and he was ready to murder Cairo, who still hadn't returned from a lunch break he'd asked her *not* to take.

"Daine? What's wrong?" Phillip frowned and walked around the counter to put a supportive arm under his elbow.

God, that felt good. He wanted to lean in, close his eyes and sleep for a week.

"I just—I think—I need a break." That wasn't what he'd planned on saying at all. *Fuck*, he didn't want to be so weak. What was wrong with him?

"I'd say you've hit the nail on the head there. I bet you haven't even taken five minutes to breathe since this morning." Phillip started pushing him towards one of the small tables. "Which reminds me — you said there was an inspection? Was it the FSIS? How did that go?"

"Don't remind me." There were three people staring at them rather than at the cupcakes they were supposedly trying to choose. "It's over and we've got 'probationary clearance', whatever that means."

"There's no such thing." Phillip shook his head. "Something weird is going on."

"Tell me about it." Daine drew back, the loss of contact with Phillip causing a stab of pain in his chest. "But right now I can't leave the counter unattended. And Cairo isn't back yet."

"She took a break and left you to it?" Phillip's frown deepened. "Something is wrong with that woman."

"I know. I need to talk to her about that." Daine sighed. He was a baker, not a people manager. He wasn't looking forward to the confrontation. "Why don't you have a cup of coffee while I serve these last few customers? I promise I'll take a break as soon as she's back."

"You better." Phillip looked towards the door with a growl, as if he could make Cairo appear by sheer force of will.

The first customer was an older lady who wanted a cupcake without *fruity bits* because her grandson hated them. Daine was about to inform her that very few, if any, of his cupcakes had *fruity bits* when Cairo walked in. If she moved any slower she would have fallen asleep.

Daine finished selling the woman some cookies and cream cupcakes, which even the grandmother admitted were very unlikely to contain any fruit. As he rang up the sale, Cairo had finally made it back behind the counter.

"Good afternoon, sir." She addressed the sombre-looking man in his forties in dark clothing who was next in line. "What would you like today?"

"I need some kosher cupcakes for my nephew's birthday party." The man cleared his throat. "He loves strawberries, but he doesn't want the pink sprinkles on top. Can you do them in blue?"

"Not a problem. I'll check for you." Cairo turned towards the kitchen and yelled, "Antonio, special order of kosher strawberry with blue frosting and sprinkles."

"Strawberries in blue?" Antonio stuck his head into the main room. "Are you sure?"

"Of course I'm sure. I'm not stupid, am I?" Cairo smirked, straightening her face before she turned back to the sombre man. "How many would you like, sir?"

"Oh, a dozen of those and a dozen chocolate should do it." The man attempted a smile, but seemed to get stuck half way.

"We make them fresh." Antonio grinned. "Will take half hour, will be quick."

Daine tore himself away. They seemed to have everything under control for now. Walking into the kitchen, he grabbed a couple of leftover slices of bread and made himself a sandwich. Carrying the plate to Phillip's table, he almost collapsed. Coffee. He was definitely going to need some of that.

"Would you like anything else?" He smiled at Phillip's relaxed pose on the chair. The man looked as if he belonged in his store.

"I'd like for you to sit down and have some food." Phillip pointed at the empty second chair. "I can walk to the kitchen and get some more coffee for us."

Daine sighed as he sat down and closed his eyes for a moment. Shit, but his life was a mess. The only good thing that had happened recently was Phillip. He didn't understand how, but he'd started caring about the man already. He shook his head. It was much too soon to read anything into what they seemed to have between them.

"Here, I've got you some coffee, just the way you like it." Phillip's warm hand on his shoulder made him open his eyes. "Two sugars and just a little milk, right?"

Damn, the man remembered how he took his coffee?

"Don't look so shocked." Phillip chuckled. "Antonio told me."

"Thank you." He inhaled the fine scent, always having believed that he was able to get his first hit of caffeine by sending it straight from his nose up into his brain. That's where he needed it most if he wanted to stand a chance of getting the fog of exhaustion he was under to lift from his brain.

With half an eye on Cairo to make sure she was doing her job, he ate his sandwich, loving the moment of relative peace and quiet. Phillip sipped his coffee and let him be until he was finished. Daine sat back and patted his belly. *Better.*

"Now, what was this about 'probationary clearance' from the health inspectors?" Phillip leant forward.

"I have no idea. They said the bakery was on probation for a month. If nothing else happens, I'll get the permanent certificate." He shrugged. "It's not like I'm going to worry about it. We've never had an incident like this before, and we'll hopefully not have one like it ever again."

"You do know that there is no such thing as 'probationary clearance', don't you?" Phillip scowled. "I'll check into it for you, if you want."

"I do know that. Let it be. I've got other things to worry about right now. And it's not like you're a lawyer or anything, is it?" God, the thought of those bloodsuckers made his skin crawl. Ever since a particularly vicious one had attacked his father, before his parents moved to Venezuela, he'd hated them with a vengeance.

His father had never said much about the case and it was all very mysterious, but it had been enough to send his parents packing. The situation must have been really serious for them to run like that, never to return. The lawyer's attacks or whatever he had done had certainly not helped.

Phillip had gone very pale and very quiet.

"What? Are you—a lawyer?" He didn't think he could bear it. "I thought you were a college professor?"

"Yes, I am." Phillip pulled himself together. "But I teach law."

"Oh." He swallowed. That was certainly close. The funny thing was that he didn't get any of the creepy, lawyerly vibes from Phillip that he usually picked up on.

"Is that a problem?" Phillip tilted his head.

"No... I don't know." Daine sighed. "Probably not."

"*Probably* not?" A small amount of colour had returned to Phillip's face. "Does that mean you're still speaking to me?"

"Yeah, I guess so." Daine shook himself. Being a law professor wasn't the same as taking horrendous sums of money from one party to go and screw the other one over in court, was it? He pushed away the thought that maybe teaching others how to do it was just as bad. He liked Phillip, damn it, and as long as the man wasn't actually involved in ruining people's lives it was okay.

"So we're still on for our date tonight?" Phillip smiled hesitantly.

"Yeah, we are." He was looking forward to it.

"Good. I can't wait." Phillip checked his watch and hissed. "And now I need to get back to the...back to work."

"Oh, before you go, I meant to ask you if any of your students might be interested in a part-time job? I urgently need help behind the counter and can't seem to find anyone who speaks enough English to be able to serve customers." Daine really wanted to take part in the Annual Cupcake Competition, but he wouldn't be able to do it if he couldn't find the time to work on his recipes.

"Um, I don't know." Phillip smiled. "But I can certainly ask. I'll put a note on the bulletin board for the first-years as well — they're usually desperate for jobs. When do you want them to start?"

"Yesterday." Daine laughed. "I need to focus on working on my competition entries, so the sooner the better. I only have until next Tuesday."

"That's less than a week! Are you sure you'll have enough time to prepare for it?" Phillip looked shocked.

"All I need to do is find some time to finalise the recipes to use. The contestants email their ingredients lists to the competition organisers the day before, their teams do the buying, and we turn up to do the baking on the day itself." It all sounded so easy when he thought about it; he was only stressed because the competition was fierce. "I can do it."

"Of course you can." Phillip had apparently recovered from his shock. "You'll need someone to start helping out in the store as soon as possible, then."

"Absolutely. The sooner, the better." He was relieved, even though no solution had been found yet. With the weekend coming up, there wasn't likely to be one any time soon, but he could hope, couldn't he?

* * * *

"Is this where I apply for the job as store assistant?"

Daine looked up from the counter he'd been cleaning to stare into the deep blue eyes of a tall girl with shoulder-length brown hair.

"Excuse me?" he pulled himself up to his full height and blinked.

"I asked if this is where I apply for the job as store assistant?" The girl shrugged. "There was a note on the bulletin board at school."

"Oh." Good, Phillip must have worked fast. "Yes, you're in the right place. I guess you're interested?"

She gave him a look as if he was stupid, then craned her neck to check out his shoes. What the hell was up with that?

"Of course you are, or else you wouldn't be here." He almost smacked his own forehead. "Let's do this again, shall we?"

"No problem." She grinned. "My name's Lilly Hasford, I'm a second-year law student and in need of a part-time job. I'd like to work here to practice my people observation skills."

"Okay, Lilly, do you have any retail experience?" *People observation skills*? Was that why she was ogling his shoes? But what did shoes have to do with observing people?

"Nope." She smiled, not concerned in the least. "But my older brother does, he's looking for a job as well, by the way, and I'm a fast learner."

"Well, at least you speak English." *Shit*, he hadn't meant to say that out loud.

Her eyebrows rose but she didn't say anything.

"Okay, I think we can give it a try. When can you start?" Assuming he hadn't scared her away.

"Right now?" She grinned, dimples forming in her cheeks. "I can do Mondays, Wednesdays and Fridays after eleven. That's just after Professor Sedgwick's class finishes. I have lectures the other days, but I can do part of the weekend, if you want."

"Let's do a trial run today, see how it goes, then we can talk details." She sounded way too good to be true. "You mentioned your brother was also looking for a job? Is he a student as well?"

"Nah, he's a freelance gardener, but he doesn't like his job. He says it's too hot outside for most of the year." She tilted her head. "He used to work in a supermarket, though, so at least he has retail experience."

"Please let him know that he can come by any time." Two potential new helpers on the same day? He owed Phillip big time.

He spent the next hour doing paperwork for Lilly's employment and showing her what she needed to know. Cairo didn't look too happy at first, but Lilly had her involved in a friendly chat quickly enough. That seemed to pacify his prickly employee a little. She should be happy about the extra help anyway.

After that he sat down at one of the small tables with a notepad, but his focus was on watching how Lilly did. She seemed to be okay dealing with all types of customers, even the picky ones. By late afternoon, he was ready to withdraw to his tiny office for a while. He needed peace and quiet to get creative. Well, that or the company of his bakers like the other night.

That made him think. He leant back in his squeaky chair, putting his feet on his desk. That peanut and tofu creation they'd made the other night had been brilliant. The savoury cupcakes were some of the bestselling in his store. What if he did a whole range of Thai-based cupcakes? Let people have their favourite takeout flavours in a different format? He bet he could come up with some great Chinese and Italian based recipes as well.

He started taking notes and had filled a few pages before he knew it.

But why stop at the main course? There were some great starters and desserts as well. Hmmm, tiramisu cupcakes. Maybe he should do a five- or six-course meal in cupcakes instead of doing different cuisines?

What he needed now was some sort of theme.

"Bye, boss." Cairo's voice startled him into checking his watch.

Holy moly, it was almost eight p.m. and time for his date with Phillip. He hadn't even once checked on Lilly. He jumped up, making the wobbly chair clatter to the floor, and stormed into the main room.

"Is she always that quick out the door?" Lilly stood with a rag in her hands, watching Cairo's backside vanish out the front door.

"I'm sorry." God, he needed to talk to Cairo about her work ethic. Not an easy discussion, but her behaviour was becoming erratic.

"Nah, it's okay. I was just wondering." Lilly started cleaning the counter, collecting the few leftover cupcakes so they could go into cold storage until tomorrow.

"You've done an outstanding job, Lilly." *Not one complaint!*

"Thank you." She grinned. "Does that mean I'm hired?"

"It certainly does. If your brother is anything like you, he'll also have a job before he knows it." And he would finally have some time to start thinking about expanding the business. If he won the competition, he'd have professionals helping him, but he bet he could open at least one more store even without their support.

"Cool. I'll let him know." Lilly was done cleaning, and she started carrying the trays into the kitchen where

Antonio and Silvio were about to finish their tasks. Daine helped and they were done in no time.

"Can you come back tomorrow and Sunday?" He wiped his hands a final time, ready to lock up behind them, race upstairs and get changed for his date.

"Sure. What time do you want me here?" Lilly picked up the purse she'd left under the counter.

"Um, if you could be here from ten to four on both days, it would be a real help." And he'd be able to continue working on his ideas for the competition.

"No problem. I'll see you tomorrow at ten." Lilly sauntered towards the door, turning around just before she left. "I like your shoes, by the way."

And with that, she was gone.

His *shoes*?

* * * *

Phillip had barely finished pinning the note he'd written for Daine to the bulletin board when his phone rang. Declan again. Man, it was Friday afternoon, and he'd hoped for some time preparing next week's classes before going home to get ready for his date with Daine. Based on their last date, they'd be unable to keep their hands off each other unless they actually made it outside. He had reservations this time, not willing to risk letting the other man starve. The experience at lunch had confirmed that Daine didn't eat enough as it was.

"Yes, Declan?" His voice sounded a lot friendlier than he felt towards his assistant. He'd never forgive Declan for talking to Mr. Arden about his increasingly personal feelings for Daine.

"Mr. Arden requires an update on the Paradis case." Declan sounded smug. "He wants it to be in person."

"Of course." *Shit,* there went his plans for a quiet afternoon. "I'm still at the college, so it'll take me a while to get back to the office. It is Friday afternoon, after all."

"What does that have to do with anything?" Declan truly had no clue.

"Most people leave their offices slightly earlier at the end of the week. Some may even have weekends away from the city planned." He sighed. "Have you never noticed that there's more traffic on a Friday?"

"Well, yes." Declan humphed. "But I never thought it was because people leave early. They really *do* that?"

Phillip rolled his eyes. The man was too focused on his job, that was for sure. Declan needed a distraction, like a hobby, or maybe a boyfriend.

"Anyway, sir, Mr. Arden is expecting you, so I won't keep you from hurrying back here." Declan ended the call.

Hurrying back there, indeed. Phillip sometimes felt like a medieval slave, at his master's beck and call at any time of day or night. Maybe working for a large firm wasn't such a good idea after all?

He made his way to his car, got in and started driving pretty much on autopilot. He didn't want to sue Daine — the man had done nothing wrong as far as he could see. All his research indicated he was a damned hard worker, and even if he had superpowers, he certainly didn't seem to be using them.

Based on the strange incident with the supposed food poisoning and the health inspection giving him a non-existent 'probationary clearance', Phillip was beginning to suspect sabotage. That, combined with Judge Sexby's revelation about Daine's father being a former Fire Judge, was pointing at someone with a grudge against the Paradis family. *That* was where Phillip wanted to focus his research next, *not* on finding evidence of non-existent wrongdoing on Daine's part.

How to tell his boss, though?

He still hadn't answered that question when he walked into the man's office.

"Mr. Sedgwick. So good of you to come into the office." Mr. Arden sat back in his chair and glared at him.

"Mr. Arden?" Sometimes silence was a good way to provoke people into saying more than they'd planned to.

"You know perfectly well that I expect an update from you." Mr. Arden's eyes were beginning to turn red. "One of the five days granted to you by Judge Sexby has already passed, and I want to know how much closer we are to getting this suspect sued."

As if the five days had been additional! They were what had been given to him initially. Only Mr. Arden's sudden need to speed things up and his lack of trust in Phillip's ability to remain objective despite the attraction he felt for Daine had tempted the man into asking for an earlier trial date.

"What I have discovered today has, in fact, confirmed my earlier suspicions about Mr. Paradis not being to blame for any abuse of superpowers at all." He held up a hand to stop his incensed boss from interrupting him. "He's still planning to participate in the Annual Cupcake Competition, which is next Tuesday, but he can't even seem to find the time to prepare for it. I've offered to help him by finding someone who can run the store for him so he has more time to focus on the competition."

"Very clever, Mr. Sedgwick." Mr. Arden seemed to relax a little. "That way it will be easier to spy on him."

"Well, I was planning on sending one of my students, so I'm afraid spying is out." That wasn't why he'd offered help in the first place, anyway.

"Doesn't matter." Mr. Arden waved his hand. "If we give him more time to focus on the competition, we're bound to come up with something we can use in court. He's not going to win with just hard work, now, is he?"

"Well, sir, I think he just might." Phillip wasn't going to let Mr. Arden forget that. "From what I've seen, this morning included, he's a very hard worker who's been exposed to some suspicious attention from the FSIS. The health inspectors behaved very strangely…"

"Mr. Sedgwick, if this man can't keep his bakery or customer eating area clean, that's no reason to excuse his abuse of superpowers." This time it was Mr. Arden who held up his hand for silence. "I am *not* paying you to find excuses, I *am* paying you to solve the problem of us finding evidence we can use in court."

There was a problem with the firm finding evidence? He'd known that was the case, but it was interesting to find his boss agreed. However, his first priority was still to try to relieve some of the pressure he was under.

"Let me ask you a question, sir." Maybe there was a way out of this with everyone saving face. "Let's just assume, for argument's sake, that there really isn't any evidence to be found."

"Impossible!" Mr. Arden moved forward in his chair, as if ready to jump up. The man definitely had an agenda. "If nothing else, this upcoming competition will provide ample opportunity to find something. And any abuse of superpowers on that grand a scale will surely warrant his arrest and punishment."

"Just bear with me, please, sir." Phillip was thinking furiously. "While I don't see any evidence of Mr. Paradis abusing his superpowers, what if I got him to agree to a withdrawal? That way there wouldn't be any illegal activity on so large a scale and we can…"

"Have you lost your mind?" Mr. Arden's face flushed red with anger. "I'm beginning to think Declan was right after all, and you have fallen under this man's spell. Let me tell you in no uncertain terms, in case you're still having trouble understanding this. You *will* find evidence against Mr. Paradis, and you will find it within the next few days. If you cannot manage this simple task, I am afraid that we're going to have to review your employment with Aden, Bainbridge, Chinook and Damek. Am I making myself clear?"

What the hell?

* * * *

Daine opened the apartment door, barely having had the time to get dressed after his quick shower. His long hair hung in wet curls, but he couldn't be bothered to run a towel over it. Seeing Phillip was a lot more urgent. God, he'd missed him, and he'd seen him only a few hours ago for lunch.

He managed to take in the vision of broad shoulders, the ripped abdomen covered by a clinging T-shirt, and muscled legs tightly encased in well-worn jeans before Phillip stepped right into his personal space and pushed him up against the wall. The man's brown eyes turned a dark chocolate hue, he buried his hands in Daine's damp hair and as Daine opened his mouth to say hello, Phillip's lips pressed against his for a scorching kiss.

Daine's hands came up around Phillip's middle and he held on, loving the heat between them, the immediate need that made him press back against Phillip's hard body to try to get as much contact as possible. He moaned into the kiss when the need to take a breath became overwhelming. He didn't want this to stop.

81

Finally, Phillip pulled back. The other man's pupils were dilated and he grinned ruefully.

"Sorry for attacking you like this, I just needed to kiss you." Phillip took a deep breath and tried to step back.

Daine wouldn't let him.

"You can attack me like that any time!" He smiled and patted Phillip's ass before letting him go. "But I think I'll dry my hair a little more, because I must admit I'd like to actually make it out of the apartment this time. I've been stuck inside all day and I'm looking forward to a change of environment."

"Oh, I've planned a change of environment for us, don't worry." Phillip closed the apartment door and pointed at the bathroom. "You go get ready, so we can kick off the evening."

Daine had rarely dried his hair so haphazardly or been ready to leave so quickly. He followed Phillip to his car and leant back in the luxury of leather seats as Phillip drove them along Turk Boulevard.

"So, where are you taking me?" Daine finally stopped watching the streets and people on various errands or on their way to dates. He turned his head, watching Phillip's strong profile as they made a left at some traffic lights.

"Somewhere we can have some fun and something to eat." Phillip's lips turned up in a smile.

"Fun and food is a good combination." Man, he was so hungry, but doing something fun with Phillip was even higher on his agenda than food.

Wasn't that the Fillmore Auditorium on their left? He looked around but they'd already gone past. He so wasn't dressed for that. But then, neither was Phillip.

"I hope you like music." Phillip made another left and they ended up in a parking lot in front of what looked like an extremely expensive spa.

"This spa has music performances?" *Very creative.*

"No, sorry." Phillip laughed and killed the engine. "But it's a good idea. I'll pass it on to them next time I'm here. You never know, you might have just invented a new trend."

"Just let me cater the cupcakes for the 'evening with music at the spa' and I'll be happy." Daine shrugged. "Not that I really need the publicity. I can hardly keep up with demand as it is."

"Let's not talk about work, please." Phillip suddenly looked very serious. "I'd like this evening to be just about us, okay?"

"Sure." What had brought that on?

Daine watched Phillip get out of the car and, before he'd shaken off his slight bewilderment about the other man's statement, Phillip opened his door for him and held out a hand. He took it gladly, ridiculously happy about the skin-to-skin contact as Phillip pulled him up before closing the door and thumbing the car locked.

They walked around a corner, past the Fillmore, and crossed the street. A historic-looking brick building with a red and blue neon sign made him gasp

"The Rasselas?" Daine was suddenly very excited. "Oh, man, I've wanted to go for ages."

"Really?" Phillip's smile was almost wider than his face.

"I love jazz, and I've never had Ethiopian food, so it seems like the perfect combination." If he got any happier he was going to start bouncing.

"You realise what the best part about Ethiopian food, at least at this place, is?" Phillip's smile turned wicked.

"No." What was the man up to? He loved surprises, and it looked like Phillip was planning another one.

"It's mostly finger foods." Phillip beamed as he opened the club's door, putting his hand in the small of Daine's back as he ushered him in first.

"Finger foods, huh?" That made his imagination go wild right there.

He was so distracted by the images of them licking each other's fingers that he didn't notice the interior decorations until they were well inside and on the way to their table. Luckily, that was in a somewhat dark corner that would afford them great views of everyone else, including the people on the dance floor, without being seen themselves. He hoped. This licking fantasy had really got him going, and not just mentally either.

Tan walls and strategically placed spotlights gave the place an earthy, yet upbeat feel. Large groups of people were milling around the bar, and some had already ventured onto the dance floor, even though it wasn't even nine p.m. yet. The music was instrumental, a jazz-blues mix Daine found very attractive. A lonely microphone in a stand indicated a singer who'd probably gone for a break.

"Wow, this is a really nice place." Daine returned his attention to Phillip, who was holding his chair for him.

"I'm glad you like it." Phillip took his seat catty-corner from him and smiled at the hostess.

She handed them each a menu and announced that their waiter, Kelile, would be right with them to take their drink orders.

"Now, let's see what damage we can do." Phillip rubbed his hands as he opened the simple three-page menu.

Daine could think of several possibilities right there. None of them doable in public, but he was hoping there'd be a private part to the evening once they were done here.

Chapter Five

"God, these sambussas are divine." Daine licked his fingers, barely stopping himself from reaching for yet another of the stuffed little triangles.

There was only one left anyway. The thin flaky crust was fried a perfect golden brown. Biting into it revealed a filling of either lentils, onions, ginger and other Ethiopian spices, or sirloin meat, scallions, chilli and nutmeg.

"Shall we share the last one?" Phillip waggled his eyebrows.

"Sure." Daine had to laugh at Phillip's antics.

Phillip took the last pastry, leant forward and held it out to him so he could take a bite. Hesitating only briefly, he sampled the delicacy, making sure his tongue touched the tip of Phillip's finger for a second. It made his eyes flare with heat. Daine responded, feeling his pants tighten. The salty flavour of Phillip's skin was almost as good as the sambussa.

"Yum." He swallowed, watching Phillip closely. "It's a lentil one."

Phillip seemed mesmerised for a moment, staring at Daine's lips. He licked them provocatively, well aware of the effect he was having. Why should he be the only one suffering from tight pants? Then Phillip shook himself into motion and devoured the other half, moaning softly as he chewed then swallowed the delicacy.

Daine leant back in his chair and enjoyed the music while they waited for Kelile to clear their dishes. Though the rhythm was lively and people were chatting and dancing, this was still a very relaxing place. He could have kicked himself for not having come here before.

"I take it you like it here?" Phillip grinned.

"Yeah, a lot. I was just thinking that I can't believe I've never been here before." He smiled, wanting to kiss the other man. "Thank you for bringing me."

"I had no idea you knew about this place, but I'm glad I picked it." One of Phillip's hands vanished under the table.

Daine felt a soft caress along his thigh. He let one of his hands follow Phillip's under the tablecloth and their fingers twined as they pretended to be fascinated by the club's goings-on. Their fingers caressing each other under the table was far more interesting, and Daine realised his hard-on was probably here to stay.

Their entrées of lamb and chicken were just as delicious as the starters had been, but what really had Daine's attention was the increasing heat between Phillip and him. Hot glances, more little caresses under the table and casual conversation soon had him so on edge that he was perfectly willing to forgo dessert to get a taste of Phillip.

That had never happened before.

He may have outgrown his hankering for cupcakes—being around them twelve hours a day had done that—but he still had a sweet tooth a mile long. So when Phillip asked him what he'd like for dessert, he caved. He'd had a peek at the menu before and remembered several tempting choices. Who in their right mind could resist baklava anyway? They'd have to be inhuman.

Traditional Ethiopian meals apparently weren't followed by a sweet treat. Instead people ate a cooling course of yogurt and cottage cheese called *lab*, or so Kelile informed them. Since the Rasselas had bowed to the American palate, offering a delectable choice of sweet dishes, they ended up ordering the baklava he'd craved.

They shared it between them, and he was relieved to discover that he, at least, had enough self-control not to want it all for himself. Phillip fed him with his fingers, and he loved the whole experience as much as the sweet stickiness. Sweet mixed just as well with the flavour of Phillip's skin as salty did. Combined with the excellent coffee which came in small espresso-sized cups, it was a worthy conclusion to their meal.

Once Phillip had paid and they were wandering back to the car, he realised how much he really didn't want the evening to end yet. He liked Phillip a lot, and their few physical encounters so far had left him wanting more.

As soon as they were inside the car Phillip turned to him.

"I had a wonderful time tonight." Phillip smiled and took his hand.

"So did I. Thank you." *Shit*, that sounded like a goodbye.

"I was kinda hoping we wouldn't have to end it yet." Phillip lifted Daine's hand and kissed each knuckle.

The man's smouldering gaze made Daine melt. Thank God he wasn't the only one wishing for more.

"Nuh-uh." *Very sophisticated, way to go.*

"Please tell me if I'm out of line here..." Phillip hesitated.

Daine shook his head, wanting perfect clarity about his reply.

"I'd like to spend more time with you, in fact, as much of the weekend as humanly possible. I know that you probably have to be back at the bakery at some point, and I promise I'll drive you there, but right now I just want to take you home with me." Phillip kept looking at him, his gaze intense.

Yes, please. Daine was all for that, but, suddenly lacking the air for a spoken response, he simply nodded. He'd deal with the getting up in the middle of the night when he had to, not a minute before.

Phillip's eyes lit up, and he had the car started and pointed back out onto the street before Daine could blink. Phillip then drove them across what seemed like half the city. They finally left the busier areas, driving along a few quiet streets with some very nice-looking condos. They were set back from the road and surrounded by well-lit little parks with trees and flowering shrubs.

Phillip turned into a smaller road that led straight into a small parking area in front of one of the more expensive buildings. Daine was impressed with the kind of money a college professor must be earning to be able to afford a place like this. Phillip held the car door for him again, and he grinned as he followed the other man into the building, past security and into the elevator.

As soon as they entered Phillip's condo on the third floor, the door barely slammed shut behind them, he was pressed against the wall in a very welcome repeat of earlier that evening. Phillip pushed a leg between Daine's, bringing their groins into suddenly much needed contact.

Phillip's chest pushed into Daine's, and finally his hot mouth touched Daine's lips. He opened up on a moan. Phillip had him panting for more and they hadn't even started to kiss yet.

While their tongues were busy trying to express what they felt, Phillip's hands dug into his hips, as if to keep him immobile. Helpless — unwilling even — to resist, Daine pushed back, creating delicious pressure on his hardening cock. Phillip groaned and deepened the kiss, his tongue sliding against Daine's with an urgency that made him want to come right then.

Finally Phillip pulled back, leaving them both panting for breath.

"Please tell me you're okay with taking this further." Phillip's eyes were huge, pupils dilated with lust. His lips were moist from their kisses and his cheeks were flushed. The man was clearly ready for more.

"I'm okay with taking this anywhere you want, provided it involves a flat surface of some kind." Daine wasn't even sure they'd need that. At this rate, he was ready for anything. Being fucked into the wall sounded as good as being fucked into the mattress, as long as Phillip was going to get on with it.

"Ungh." Phillip's hips bucked before his grip on Daine's hips tightened as he struggled to get himself back under control. "You're my kind of man, honey!"

Phillip stepped back, took his hand and started walking towards the right. Daine was so focussed on watching Phillip's profile and feeling his hand touching his skin, he only vaguely noticed the hallway they walked along, passing two doors. Phillip pushed open the third and Daine tore his attention away so he could at least see where the bed was.

It was huge—more than a king size—made of dark wood, and took up a good part of the room. Dark green covers matched the carpet, and there were two nightstands. That was as much as he got in the few seconds Phillip left him before pulling him back into his arms. The kiss that followed took Daine's breath away. Phillip's tongue took his mouth without any hesitation, making him grind his hips against him with increasing urgency. He was now almost painfully hard.

"Too many clothes." Daine wanted skin so badly, he managed to tear himself away for the few seconds it took to take his T-shirt off.

Phillip followed his example, revealing his muscled chest with dark brown nipples. Best of all, he had a covering of dark, slightly curly hair. Daine couldn't resist and reached out so he could run his fingers through it. It was so soft. His caresses made Phillip moan and temporarily stopped his efforts to open his pants.

Daine forced himself back, focusing on getting the rest of his clothes off, leaving everything in an untidy heap right next to where he stood. When he looked up, Phillip was naked as well and they spent a few moments visually exploring each other's bodies.

Man, Phillip was built. And beautiful. He looked like a superhero with his broad shoulders, small waist and strong thighs. His milk-chocolate brown skin gave him an exotic touch, making Daine want to lick him all over.

Phillip held out a hand, took Daine's in his and moved him towards the bed. The cover was quickly pulled back and Phillip's sudden tug on his arm surprised him into falling onto the sheets, bouncing slightly on the soft mattress. Breathless from the surprise action, he laughed, crawling into Phillip's open arms to snuggle up to all that naked skin from chest to groin. Legs entangling, they returned to kissing. Only this was a lot better. Daine let his hands roam across the warm, naked skin, feeling the muscles move underneath.

Phillip's hands were equally inquisitive, stroking his flanks, up his sides and along his back. When one reached his nape and made small circles there, Daine was in heaven. He pushed up against Phillip, trying to get even closer.

"Want you." Daine's voice was husky, focusing on words difficult.

"The feeling is mutual," Phillip whispered.

Daine buried his nose in Phillip's neck, taking a deep breath. God, the man smelt wonderful. Daine licked the soft skin behind Phillip's ear and, to his delight, it caused Phillip to moan.

"God, you're driving me mad with need." Phillip tightened his grip around Daine's middle then slid his hand lower, cupping an ass cheek.

Not quite where Daine wanted him yet, but he was getting there. Daine pushed back into the warm hand on his buttock, trying to communicate what he wanted. Phillip got the message and slid a finger between his ass cheeks, exploring downward along the crease until he reached Daine's hole.

Fuck, that felt good.

"Like this?" Phillip's smile was impish.

"More!" Daine pushed back, trying to get that tempting finger inside him. It wasn't what he really wanted, but it was a start.

"Not without lube, baby." Phillip's finger vanished.

The man stretched, reached for a drawer in the closest nightstand and pulled out a bottle of lube and a foil packet.

Much better.

"You want to put this on me?" Phillip handed him the condom.

"With pleasure." Daine took the package, opened it and slid the rubber onto Phillip's engorged penis.

He stroked up and down the beautiful member a few times, just to see the other man's face melt into delighted enjoyment and to hear him moan. Phillip enjoying pleasure was a sight to behold. Daine filed his earlier idea of licking the man from top to bottom away under *definitely going to happen*. He couldn't wait to drive Phillip absolutely crazy.

A slicked finger made its way across his hole. *Shit.* He'd been too distracted to notice what Phillip was up to, and now it was his turn to express his arousal. Phillip withdrew his hand—was he ever going to penetrate? With a small push against his shoulder, Phillip motioned him onto his back.

His legs spread of their own accord when Phillip's hand started travelling up his leg, along the inside of his thigh and back between his ass cheeks. Finally Phillip gave him what he wanted. Gripping Phillip's free hand for support, Daine bore down as the slicked finger pushed inside, teasing the sensitive skin and making him pant with increased arousal. Another two fingers later, he was ready to hit the ceiling with need.

"Please." He could hardly speak. "Need you inside me."

Phillip nodded and moved between Daine's legs.

Daine slid his hands behind his knees, pulling his legs further apart and up. Phillip put a hand next to Daine's shoulder, using the other to guide the tip of his cock to Daine's hole.

Phillip looked straight into Daine's eyes as he pushed into his body. Daine's muscles stretched, the slight burn only increasing his arousal. It had been a while, but the feeling of Phillip slowly sliding inside was better than anything he'd ever felt before.

When Phillip was all the way inside, his soft balls pressed against Daine's skin, he let go of his legs and slid them around Phillip's hips. He used his hands to pull his lover closer for a kiss. He found Phillip's tongue ready for him and they caressed and stroked each other for a while in an exploration that made him eager to feel Phillip move. In fact, he soon became desperate for motion.

Without breaking the kiss, Phillip pulled out, then slowly thrust back inside. Man, that felt just right.

"Yes!" He held onto Phillip's broad shoulders as he pushed up the next time Phillip thrust into his tingling channel.

"God, you're tight." Phillip's forehead was soon covered in a thin layer of sweat as he started fucking Daine with increasing speed. "Perfect."

He nodded, too excited to speak. Phillip was the perfect one here, but he didn't have the breath to say so. He met Phillip's thrusts with more and more force, his need to come making his skin feel too tight. He was so aroused, he was about to come without even touching himself.

"Shit. Gonna!" Phillip panted, his thrusts becoming erratic.

"Yeah." Daine tightened his sphincter, trying to make it even better for both of them. It wasn't going to be long now.

"You first." Phillip straightened his arms.

"Fuck." Daine thought he was going to die from bliss.

Phillip started really pounding into him. The strength of his thrusts made the bed shake and Daine trembled with anticipation. A slight shift in Phillip's angle and his lover squarely hit his prostate on the next few strokes. That was it, it was all over.

"Phillip!" Daine came in long bursts of pleasure, his semen splattering his chest and abdomen as his orgasm made him see stars.

Phillip's eyes widened as he lost his rhythm, stiffened and filled the condom as his entire body shook with the strength of his release. The sight and sounds made Daine's delightfully stretched hole twitch, and his spent cock dribbled out a few more drops of cum as the final aftershocks made him sigh.

Phillip collapsed on top of him, the man's weight making for welcome reassurance that Daine was still alive.

"Man, that was something else." Daine tightened his arms when Phillip started to pull out.

If he never left, it would be too soon. But the reality of having to deal with the condom took precedence, so — reluctantly — he let Phillip go. He was back in record time and cleaned him up with a warm washcloth before dropping it unceremoniously onto the floor next to the bed and falling back into his arms.

"You're amazing, baby." Phillip nuzzled between his neck and his shoulder, settling the rest of his long body against him.

"Um-hm. You too." His eyes already closed, Daine smiled.

This was a very promising beginning to what he'd hoped would be a fun weekend. It looked like his wish was about to come true.

* * * *

Phillip yawned. God, it had been a glorious weekend. Once again he was on his way into the office, trying to keep his eyes open. Monday morning had come much too quickly. He wanted it to be Friday night all over again.

Not that he'd survive another three nights with mind-blowing sex and almost no sleep. Driving Daine back to the bakery before four a.m., and a few short naps taken during the daytime while trying to catch up with work. It just wasn't enough.

How did Daine survive on so little sleep? He did it so well, too. The man looked great, clearly kept fit, had endless supplies of energy, and in bed? He was a true tiger.

Phillip grinned. It made him want to spend even more time with him, but that wasn't going to happen for at least another week or so.

First, there was the big Cupcake Competition on Tuesday. Personally, he hoped Daine would do really well. Professionally, he knew it was going to get the man into even more trouble. If he won the competition, Mr. Arden would see it as final proof that Daine was indeed guilty.

Then there was the trial in the Fire Court, which was still scheduled for Wednesday. He doubted there was anything or anyone who could move that date or make the trial go away. Everything he had seen and heard from those higher up indicated that someone was very interested in seeing Daine convicted for his alleged abuse of superpowers.

Phillip snorted. He had yet to see any indication of any superpowers at all, never mind ones originating with Daine. As much time as he'd spent with him, he was now sure the man wasn't using any superpowers at all. Mr. Arden's insistence that Daine was guilty looked increasingly weird in light of the total lack of evidence Phillip had found. Downright suspicious, in fact.

Maybe it was time to examine Mr. Arden's possible motives for wanting Daine found guilty. There'd been a few hints, but he hadn't followed up on any of them so far because he'd wanted to make sure Daine was innocent. Now, it was time to look for evidence elsewhere. He was going to start with a look into Mr. Arden's background, but the mysterious reasons for Daine's father's fall from grace that Judge Sexby had mentioned might lead to the truth of what was going on as well. As for the judge's role in all of this? Phillip was ready for anything.

He couldn't shake the feeling that somewhere, someone was pulling strings to set Daine up for a totally undeserved fall. Was it because of Daine's father? Were they trying to get him out of hiding? Was something even more sinister going on?

Still occupied with his thoughts, he walked into his office on autopilot. When he looked up, Mr. Damek was sitting in his visitor's chair. Calm and unruffled, dressed in his signature brown suit and green shirt, the man just by being there almost gave Phillip a heart attack. Partners didn't normally appear in junior employees' offices.

"Can I—can I help you?" Phillip set his briefcase down in its usual place next to his desk, considering whether it was better to remain standing or whether he was expected to sit down.

"That all depends." Mr. Damek smiled, somehow managing to make it an expression of slight disapproval.

Great! The man was presenting riddles and Phillip hadn't even had coffee yet.

"Don't worry, this isn't going to take long." Mr. Damek leant forward. "But it's essential that you listen to me. You're in quite some danger of not only ruining your career with this firm, but losing your life in the process."

"My life?" That made Phillip sit down, hard.

"Yes, your life." All traces of a smile were gone from Mr. Damek's face. "There are forces at work in your current case that are way beyond your control."

"*Forces*?" Just what he needed.

"I'm surprised your boss hasn't warned you." Mr. Damek shook his head, his medium-length brown hair not moving at all. "Ignatius is well known for his love of risk, but frankly, I think this is going too far."

"What is going on here?" Mr. Arden's voice boomed from the entrance to Phillip's office.

"We were having a friendly chat." Mr. Damek seemed unruffled, but he got up and walked towards the door, his willingness to share clearly gone.

"A friendly chat, huh?" Mr. Arden frowned at the other partner and stepped back to let him leave.

"Nothing to be concerned about." Mr. Damek looked back at Phillip. "Just remember what I said and you'll be fine."

Phillip grimaced as both men left the office together, headed towards the Monday morning partners' meeting. Mr. Arden was talking in low tones, clearly trying to get more information out of Mr. Damek. From his increasingly angry expression, it didn't look like he was having any luck.

What the hell is going on here?

* * * *

The chaos was indescribable. The competition commission had taken over several large hotel kitchens across the city. The one Daine was in had ingredients all over the counters, bowls and cooking implements in various stages of use and panicked helpers running around between cooking stations, trying to solve any last-minute panics. Of which there had been a few.

Daine looked over his shoulder before taking a step back, carefully balancing the baking tray with his finished cupcakes. There weren't just the other contestants to look out for, but there were reporters and cameras everywhere as well. He didn't remember there ever being such a ridiculous media circus before.

He sighed as he pushed the tray into the pre-heated industrial oven at the back wall. There were seven contestants in his group, all trying to outdo each other. There were eight groups like this in all. Once the winners for each of the eight groups had been determined, there would be a second round in the afternoon at another location to determine the final three contestants. The chances of him winning were lower than he cared to think about, but he had to try.

Closing the oven, he stepped back and wiped his hands. He had just under twenty minutes to finish the icing for his Thai menu selection. His concept had been well received by the judges, receiving the full ten points for Originality and nine out of ten for Customer Interest. One of the highest rankings in his group, but he had no idea what was going on in the other seven groups. That wouldn't be revealed until this afternoon, together with the winners from round one.

While he'd made three basic sets of cupcake batter — rice-, noodle- and tofu-based, respectively — the icing was going to add more of the variation you'd see on a Thai menu. He lovingly added flavours and natural colours to the small bowls he'd prepared earlier, making sure the finishing decorations he'd use were ready next to their respective containers.

"This looks like quite an unusual setup for cupcakes." The voice came from straight behind him.

"What?" Daine had been focusing on making the peanut sprinkles just the right size.

He turned around to check who was interrupting him. Of course, it was a reporter, hair askew and little recording device at the ready. Why didn't these people understand that the contestants needed to focus on what they were doing? He wasn't here for everyone's entertainment. He was here to win the contest.

"I was thinking that your idea of a Thai menu is rather unusual." The guy shook his head.

What was he supposed to say to that? Why did the guy feel like he needed to comment anyway? Daine shrugged and returned to his work. The distraction had only cost him less than a minute, but the stress it caused stayed with him for a while.

Finally the oven signalled that the dough was done. He pulled the baking sheet out and set it onto the counter for the cupcakes to cool off. The scent was already fantastic, and the colourful decorations would only increase his production's appeal.

The nosy reporter from earlier was still around, watching his every move as if waiting for some catastrophe to happen. What was wrong with this guy?

Daine returned to finishing the cupcakes by adding the vegetable-flavoured icing and pieces of decoration. Once they were done, he started transferring them into the large flat basket with a two-inch border he'd chosen. Earlier, he'd covered the bottom with banana leaves so everything was ready for the cupcakes to be stuck on with a small dollop of icing each.

When he was done, the presentation plate looked like a veritable feast of Thai dishes. They definitely looked appealing and exotic. Everything from vegetables to fruit for the sweet and sour dishes, small prawns and diced pieces of chicken indicated the flavour to be expected from any given cupcake.

He carefully transferred his basket to the long table that had been set aside for the judges to walk along. He found the little sign with his entry number and set the basket down. Now all there was left to do was watch and wait.

"Impressive." The first judge, an older woman wearing reading glasses, took a photograph with a small digital camera. "What inspired you to come up with your concept of a Thai menu?"

"I, well, I really like Thai food." *Shit, could he sound any more moronic?* "So the other night, when we had Thai takeout for dinner, we just got into experimenting with different flavours."

"We being you and…" The woman looked over her glasses, making him feel like he was back in school.

"My colleagues." He smiled, trying to look relaxed. "We sometimes experiment like that, and, in this case, it gave me the idea for my competition entry."

"Fascinating." The woman stared at the different varieties for a long minute, taking each one in and making copious notes on her clipboard.

God, he hoped they were complimentary.

With a final nod she passed on to the next contestant's presentation. It looked like a kaleidoscope of colours, neither rhyme nor reason to it other than it being extremely colourful and sickeningly sweet looking.

It didn't take long for the tasting judges to make their way over to his spot. The older man's eyes lit up when he saw Daine's offerings, and the younger man even smiled. That was bound to be a good sign, right?

Both judges sampled three cupcakes each, drinking sips of water from plastic cups in-between changing flavours. They didn't say anything, but wore smiles on very happy faces when they wrote down their thoughts. They nodded at him before passing on to the other participants.

Daine had never been so nervous. He anxiously watched the three judges as they made their way around the table holding the entries. There were quite a few very nice-looking cupcake creations in all colours of the rainbow. Most of them looked traditional and sweet. He was beginning to worry that his concept of savoury cupcakes might be too far out there when the judges made their last notes and withdrew to a separate room to discuss their verdict.

It was too late to change anything anyway. He went to get himself a cup of coffee and sat down in the hotel's dining room, where all the contestants were either being harassed by reporters or sitting quietly, chewing their nails and looking nervous.

He wished Phillip could be with him. The man had such a calming influence upon him. Well, when he wasn't making him totally hot. When they'd talked about work and his plans for the store, the other man had listened intently, as if he was really interested. He'd been encouraging about the competition, once his initial surprise had been over. And sending one of his students to help out in the bakery had been such a godsend.

Hopefully, they'd be able to get together tonight. He was looking forward to each date. Whether he won the competition or not, he wanted to feel Phillip's arms around him, kissing him senseless, and maybe even spend the night.

God, he had it bad.

After an indeterminable time, the judges finally emerged from their seclusion and proceeded to sit at the table at the front of the room. Several rows of chairs were lined up facing them, and everyone took a seat. Daine, as a contestant, had a seat in the first row.

"Welcome to the final part of round one of the third Annual Cupcake Competition." The woman had taken the lead, smiling at each participant in turn. "This has been a particularly challenging contest to judge so far, and we don't anticipate it becoming any easier as the day progresses. Only one of the contestants will make it into the second round, and we anticipate the competition to be even steeper this afternoon."

Man, he'd been nervous anyway. This didn't help him relax in the least.

"So, without further ado, we will announce the winners of this first round." The judge picked up a sheet of paper and glanced at it. "In third place, for a cash prize of one hundred dollars, is Mozart's Bakery."

A thin redhead rose to polite applause to collect his certificate and cheque.

"In second place, for a cash prize of five hundred dollars, is the owner of the Tao Bakery. We were particularly impressed by her outstanding bitter chocolate icing." The judge handed a woman who looked like a gypsy her prize.

"And now, the moment you have all been waiting for." The judge took a final look at her sheet before raising her gaze. "In first place, for a cash prize of one thousand dollars and the right to advance to the second and final round, is the gentleman who impressed us all with his creativity and novel concept."

Daine took a deep breath. Had he heard right?

"Mr. Daine Paradis, owner of Fabulous Cupcakes, will you please come forward?" The woman smiled at him, beckoning him forward.

The applause sounded loud in his ears as he rose and walked forward. *Wow*. He'd done it. He'd made it into the final round.

Shit. That meant he had to go through the same stress again this afternoon.

"Well done." The judge handed him a certificate, a cheque and a new entrant's badge. "The second round will start at two p.m., in The Fairmont. Good luck!"

"Thank you." Daine took everything, still in a daze.

When he turned around, the ever-present reporters were already juggling for the best position for an interview. Oh, well, it was all part of the game. It couldn't even faze him for now.

He'd made it into the second round! He couldn't wait to tell Phillip.

Chapter Six

Surprisingly, Phillip hadn't had a call from Declan to come back to the office after his Tuesday morning lecture. He had only today left before the trial, and the lack of interest from Mr. Arden indicated he'd either given up or, more likely, was planning something else to bring Daine down. So Phillip had decided to do his digging into who might be behind this campaign against Daine, using his college office and computer. It made more sense to do it away from the office anyway — you never knew who or what was being monitored there.

That his boss was after his lover was now certain beyond the shadow of a doubt. Phillip sat at his cluttered desk and stared at the computer screen as if it was going to bite him.

Fuck!

It was amazing what information the Internet would reveal if you knew where to look. A bit of clever searching and hacking here and there, and some secret databases had yielded some interesting facts. None of which were going to make his job easier, or help Daine in the immediate future.

Double fuck!

Apparently, Daine's family was a mess. None of the sparse research Declan had come up with had indicated anything close to this number of issues. Phillip filed this bit of information away for later use. There was more going on with Declan than met the eyes, and none of it good.

Focusing back on Daine's situation would keep him occupied for quite a while. He now knew that a long-standing rivalry between Daine's father and his uncle seemed to have been the cause for Daine's parents moving to Venezuela three years ago. They hadn't been heard of since, which was interesting. Few people managed to vanish so completely. Phillip wondered whether Judge Sexby, who'd told him that Daine's father had been a Fire Judge, knew what was going on. Not that he could ask him.

But that wasn't what had him so upset. Daine's uncle, one Gascon Paradis, had tried to take the bakery from Daine, who had refused to sell. Various financial shenanigans ensued, none of which had been successful. Then, about two years ago, the uncle, too, had vanished. There were some links to mysterious organisations, but nothing Phillip could put his finger on.

What little he had found out about them had him very nervous. Some of their members were suspected superpower criminals, while others were people who hadn't quite made the grade when being tested for membership in the official Association of Superheroes. All of them had reason to hate the existing superpower establishment.

If these were the people Daine's uncle had allied himself with, in what Phillip assumed to be some sort of crusade for revenge, Daine was in real trouble. *They* could have been the ones using superpowers to make it look as if Daine was to blame. Exposing them before the trial took place tomorrow, without any kind of evidence, was going to be impossible.

Double fuck with a cherry on top.

He was going to have to tell Daine what was going on, so the man could protect himself. He was also going to make sure Daine's lawyer was someone competent to defend his lover. If Phillip left it up to the system, or whoever was pulling the strings here, Daine was sure to end up with an incompetent fool.

His phone rang and he jumped from the shock of being pulled back into reality. His office was already half dark, the sun outside about to set. He'd been here a lot longer than he'd planned. Checking caller ID made him sigh with relief. It was Daine.

"Hey, babe. How are you?" Phillip wasn't going to ask how it went, but the fact that Daine hadn't called earlier in the day surely meant he'd at least made it to the second round.

"I need to see you, please." Daine sounded neutral, as if he was holding something back.

"Sure." Shit, maybe his assumption had been wrong and Daine needed consoling? "Where do you want to meet?"

"I feel like a quiet night at home." Daine swallowed. "I hope you don't mind?"

"Of course not." That didn't sound good at all. "I'm still at the college, so I'll only be a few minutes."

"No, actually I meant my real home, my apartment in Nob Hill. My roommates are out of town, so we'll have the place to ourselves." Daine proceeded to give him directions.

He took careful notes, mindful of his temperamental GPS. He said goodbye, closed down his computer and shoved a few printouts into his briefcase, just in case. He'd need some sort of proof, ambiguous as it was, when he told Daine what was going on.

Phillip made it to Daine's apartment in record time. Thank God the traffic was with him for once. He made it into the building thanks to another resident leaving to walk their dog by catching the door just as it was about to fall shut. He ran up the stairs to the seventh floor, unwilling to wait for the elevator.

There was a sticky note with a tiny picture of a cupcake right next to the doorbell. *Come on in, the door's open.* Shit, he was going to have to talk to Daine about security.

Intrigued, he opened the door, went inside, carefully locked it behind him and put down his briefcase. The apartment was quite large, with wooden floors as far as he could see from the entrance through to the living room and an open kitchen on the left. There was a shadowed hallway to the right, presumably leading to the bedrooms.

"Daine?"

Silence was his only response.

Looking for further directions he discovered a trail of yummy looking cupcakes starting about five feet from where he stood. He laughed. That was so Daine! They led his eye to the third door on the right, which was ajar.

Bingo.

He was very tempted to pick up the cupcakes — they looked too good to be left on the floor and used as simple markers. But the feeling that something else was going on here and the need to see Daine as quickly as possible won out. He followed where the cupcakes led and slowly pushed open the bedroom door.

Seconds was all he had to take in the decor, and all of that was forgotten as soon as he noticed Daine. The other man was totally naked, on his back, legs spread wide on the comforter of a double bed. The view of his lover slowly stroking his clearly very hard cock took Phillip's breath away. The speed of his blood travelling south as his body responded made him dizzy.

"I've been waiting for you." Daine smiled and held out his hand.

"I was hoping you'd say that." *Fuck work and all the other issues.* Phillip started tearing off his clothes, leaving them in a chaotic trail behind him on the floor as he made his way over to the bed.

Daine opened his arms and Phillip moved next to him, sliding his hands along all that naked skin as he moved so their cocks were touching. He lowered his mouth to take a taste of his lover. Lips met and tongues duelled as he moved closer, rubbing Daine's length with his own.

"Missed you." Daine had pulled back to get some air.

"Yeah." Phillip wasn't ready to stop his exploration of Daine's sweet lips and mouth. He dove right back in, kissing his lover until he felt faint and had to pull back.

"I love your kisses." Daine's smile was sweet and his eyes large in his very flushed face.

They were both panting for breath. Daine's scent was heady, a faint leftover of soap telling Phillip he'd recently taken a shower. Nobody had ever got Phillip this excited in so short a time. He lifted his hand to cup Daine's face. He was about to say how much the other man was beginning to mean to him when he stopped short. God, they'd only known each other for a week, it was way too soon.

Daine nuzzled into Phillip's hand, closing his eyes.

"I want you," Daine whispered, "...please."

"You can have me any way you like." *Fuck*, but that pleading look just before Daine had closed his eyes had gone straight to his heart.

His hips bucked as his arousal increased. He'd never liked the thought of a man having to beg to be made love to, but he had to admit it had a certain appeal when Daine did it. Daine stretched and pulled open the nightstand drawer. Pulling out a bottle of lube and a condom wrapper, he placed both into Phillip's hand. Sheathing himself quickly, he pushed a lube-covered finger along Daine's crack, rubbing circles around the tiny hole until Daine moaned.

"More." Daine pushed back, trying to capture his finger.

Phillip stopped moving to watch his lover take the digit right inside the tight heat. He had to take a deep breath to fight for control. The sight of Daine fucking himself on first one finger, then two and finally three would make him come if he wasn't careful.

Daine whimpered.

It was time. Pulling out, he turned onto his back and motioned Daine to straddle him.

"Ride me, baby." Phillip's voice was close to a growl.

Daine's eyes widened, but he lifted his ass, reached behind him and put Phillip's cock right where they both wanted it. Apparently not willing or able to wait another second, he sank down until Phillip was balls-deep inside him.

"Fuck!" That was the best feeling ever.

Daine grinned and started to move. Sleek muscles playing under his skin, he lifted himself all the way up, then pushed back down with a sigh.

"Yes!" Daine's face was contorted in pleasure as he leant forward to support himself by placing his hands on Phillip's chest.

Phillip took hold of his lover's hips and helped him move. When Daine started making little circles with his hips as he fucked himself on Phillip's cock, he knew it wasn't going to take much longer. The feeling was unbelievable. The view of a now sweat-covered Daine taking his pleasure like that drove him so close to the edge that he had to bite his lips to distract himself from coming.

He lifted a hand to enclose Daine's cock and his lover whimpered again. Phillip decided he liked that sound and started stroking the other man's cock in earnest.

A strangled cry was his response as Daine started coming. The smell of his semen as it hit his chest was the final straw. Phillip pushed back into Daine's clenching hole with one last thrust and came so hard he saw stars.

Daine held on until he was done, then he pulled off, dealt with the condom and collapsed half on, half off Phillip. The sound of them trying to catch their breath was loud in the quiet room. Phillip tightened his arm around his lover and held him close.

"Wow." Phillip didn't want to move ever again.

"Yeah." Daine's grin was infectious.

"So, what's with all the cupcakes?" He just hoped they were a good sign.

"They're leftovers." Daine didn't move a muscle.

"From what?" Was the man going to make him pull every single word out of him like this?

"My victory." Daine's lips definitely twitched this time.

"You *won*?" Phillip crushed Daine to him and covered his face in kisses. "That's perfect, baby. God, I'm so *happy* for you."

"Thank you." Daine's smile could have lit a city for a year. "It was apparently a close call, but in the end my 'Thai menu' convinced the judges."

"Wow, that's amazing." Phillip desperately tried to push any and all thoughts of the possible consequences to the back of his mind.

"What's wrong?" Daine frowned.

God, was the man that sensitive?

"I just..." There was no point in lying. Especially not since he'd made up his mind he'd have to tell his lover what was going on anyway. But how the hell was he going to do it?

"Something *is* wrong." Daine tried to pull back.

Phillip didn't want to let him go, but they were probably better off dressed and not distracted by each other's nakedness.

"Well, yes and no." Phillip put his finger across Daine's lips to stop the man from protesting. "There are a few things I need to tell you, and I think we should have a quick shower and get dressed before we get into it."

"Okay." Daine's worried look almost broke Phillip's heart.

"It's nothing that needs to affect us, baby." Phillip was afraid that it would, what with Daine's dislike of lawyers he remembered.

But he desperately hoped it wouldn't push them apart. Daine would need all the support he could get, and Phillip was more than willing to give him that — even to the detriment of his own career. What Mr. Arden wanted him to do, especially in the light of his newest findings, just wasn't right.

* * * *

Daine was shaking with nerves. He stuffed his T-shirt into the shorts he'd hastily grabbed from a drawer before taking his turn in the shower, then looked in the mirror. His curly hair had gone even curlier with the moisture in the bathroom and needed a good brushing. But all he had time for was a quick finger-comb and pulling it back into a somewhat messy ponytail. *Shit*, but he needed to find out what was wrong with Phillip.

Phillip had taken a seat on the sofa in the living room and patted the spot next to him as soon as Daine entered the room. With a relieved sigh, he sank next to his lover and took the offered hand. At least the man was still friendly, so surely it couldn't be too bad?

"I've got a few things I need to tell you, and I'd like it very much if you'd give me the chance to finish my part of the story before commenting." Phillip took a deep breath. "Some of this will sound weird, some of it you'll hate, but I'd like you to remember that, whatever it sounds like, I'm on *your* side."

"There are sides?" Daine leant back against the sofa for support. "That sounds serious, like there's a fight or something."

He'd thought he was joking, but the stricken look on Phillip's face convinced him that he was close to the truth. *What the hell?*

"It's beginning to look that way, yes." Phillip frowned. "I didn't realise until this afternoon, when I finally did some background research, but it seems that your family has some issues, or problems, that have resulted in a split into two camps."

"My father and my uncle." Daine felt all the colour drain from his face. "Are they at it again?"

"They've been 'at it' before?" Phillip raised his eyebrows.

"I don't know any details. Nobody ever told me what was going on. But I remember they got into terrible fights when I was smaller. Then they didn't talk for years, and when my parents moved to Venezuela three years ago I wanted to take over the business. My father agreed at first. Then there was a big fight with my uncle. Once I had ownership, he offered to buy the business from me." It had been a lot more than an offer, actually.

"But you didn't sell?" Phillip tilted his head, clearly interested.

"Hell, no." He shook his head. "The bakery was my father's dream. Uncle Gascon never supported my dad when times were tough, never even took any interest. And suddenly he wanted to take over? Claiming I was too young and inexperienced to run it by myself? Not likely!" He paused. "I made some pretty hefty payments to my father for it." He shook his head as if to forget the experience.

"I'm glad you resisted. You're doing a wonderful job with it, and your winning the competition today only proves it." Phillip smiled and squeezed his hand.

"So where's the problem?" Daine's eyes widened. "I haven't heard from my uncle in two years... Oh, God, is he trying to come back and take over again?"

"Not directly, at least that I can see." Phillip looked at the floor, as if to collect his thoughts before returning his gaze to Daine. "This is going to sound weird, but it seems that he has allied himself with some very strange and possibly unscrupulous people. I have no proof as yet, but it looks as though they're supporting him in his bid to get you removed as owner of the bakery."

"How?" Had his uncle been planning this for the last two years? Was that why he'd vanished? Was that the explanation for all the weird mishaps with deliveries of supplies over the last few months? Not to mention the break-ins?

"This is going to sound strange, but bear with me. I'll try and explain it all." Phillip leant back. "How much do you know about your father's activities outside of running the bakery?"

"Huh? He had time for anything other than the shop?" Daine chewed his lip.

Now that he thought of it, he'd been away at college most of the time, so he might not have noticed.

"Yes, he did. Has he ever mentioned to you that there are certain — talents in your family?" Phillip definitely looked uncomfortable.

"Talents? As in my father's ability to bake?" Surely that wasn't anything out of the ordinary? There were lots of very talented bakers all over the world.

"That's the one. Except it's more than a talent. He probably never told you this, but that 'talent' is actually one of many well-known superpowers." Phillip stared at him intently.

"Superpowers?" He wanted to laugh, but Phillip's statement hadn't sounded like a joke, and there was no other indication that Phillip was joking. "Are you serious?"

"Very." Phillip nodded. "Your father's power is linked to the elemental power of fire, hence his capability to bake. Examples of some of the other powers linked to fire are smithing, metalworking and some forms of healing. There are three other elemental types of power, such as earth, which results in an ability to deal well with everything linked to plants and animals. Then there are water and air powers, but those details aren't important right now."

"Superpowers?" Daine felt as if the floor had been pulled out from under his feet. Was that the explanation why he'd been so successful? But he wasn't conscious of doing anything other than working hard. "And my uncle has them, too?"

"I don't know yet." Phillip shrugged. "I've been trying to find out, but, from what I've seen, his powers are either non-existent or very weak, or he would have taken the bakery from you when your parents left. That's why I suspect he has allied himself with someone who is using powers illegally—"

"Hold on." Daine lifted his hand for emphasis. "If you say there are illegal uses of those so called superpowers—that means there are legal ones as well?"

"Yes." Phillip nodded. "And I work for a firm that protects the legal use of superpowers."

"You work...doing what?" Daine narrowed his eyes, a horrible suspicion taking shape in his mind.

"My job as a professor of law at the college is only part of what I do. Mostly I'm a lawyer." Phillip shrank back.

"A *lawyer*?" Daine felt the blood drain from his brain, and not in a good way. "You mean you take money from people to...what? Accuse others?"

"Not really." Phillip rubbed his temples.

"So, what *do* you do?" God, he didn't want Phillip to be like the lawyer who'd made his parents go away. "Were you involved in the case which forced my father to leave? The one he never told me anything about?"

"That's a whole lot of questions, and of course I'll try to answer all of them." Phillip got up and started to pace. "First of all, there's usually no money involved. My firm works for the Superpower Court, much like public prosecutors in the US legal system. We do occasionally get hired by private individuals, but that's very rare."

"Okay." That didn't sound too bad. "What about my parents' case?"

"I've only been working for Arden, Bainbride, Chinook and Damek for about six months, so I wasn't involved in your parents' case." Phillip stopped moving and stared at him. "As far as I was able to determine, someone did hire that lawyer you referred to so it looked as though there was a US legal case, but in fact there was something going on behind the scenes."

"Meaning it was linked to my father's alleged superpower?" Daine shook his head. This was all a bit much to take in. But Phillip didn't look like a crazy person who'd make all of this up either.

"As far as I know, it was." Phillip sighed and sat back down. "This is where I tell you the reason for my interest in all this. Someone has made an accusation against you, alleging you're using superpowers to make your store a success."

"Who?" It had to have been his uncle.

"I don't know for sure, but now that I know he was after your bakery three years ago, I suspect it may have been your uncle." Phillip rubbed his temples again. "It could have been someone else, but, whoever it is, they're putting a lot of pressure on my boss, Mr. Arden, to get you convicted by the Fire Court."

"The Fire Court? Get me convicted?" Shit, he hadn't done anything wrong. "But I don't even have any superpowers!"

"I agree." Phillip nodded.

Daine felt his fury bubbling up inside him.

"All my life, my dad told me if I worked hard and was good to others and played by the rules and paid my taxes…I could—and would—succeed. I work hellish, long days. I call that working hard. If that's me tweaking some kind of superpower, then I must really be an extremely lousy magician!"

"This isn't about magic. That has nothing to do with what we're talking about." Phillip looked so serious when he said this, it had to be true. "This is about elemental superpowers that have existed since the beginning of time. It may look like magic to some, and probably gets mistaken for magic by those who don't understand, but the source of these powers lies in natural forces linked to the Earth itself. So please, sweetheart, relax."

"Relax? I'm about to lose everything." Daine started pacing now, aware of Phillip's anguished gaze. "If there's a trial, I need a defence attorney, don't I?"

Phillip shrugged. "Someone to defend you at the very least, but, yes, a good attorney would be best."

"Holy crap. I could lose everything." His knees felt weak. He'd fought so hard, had finally won the Annual Cupcake Competition and was about to get professional support to expand his business — and now this!

"I'm not going to let them throw you under the bus, Daine. I've found no evidence of wrongdoing. I see how hard you work." He leaned closer to him. "Didn't you get the warning notices? In red envelopes on your bakery door? According to my case files, you've been sent far more than a dozen."

"Red envelopes?" Daine had no idea what Phillip was talking about. "Never. Not one."

"That's so weird. The court must, by spiritual law, give you monthly warnings."

God. Please tell me I'm gonna wake up and find it's all a dream.

"So you've been looking for evidence that I'm using superpowers?" He felt all his hopes for his relationship with Phillip vanish.

"That's how it started, yes." Phillip held up a hand to stop him from interrupting. "But that's not why I stuck around. I really like you, and I want to do anything I can to help you out of this mess."

"You do?" God, he wanted that to be true. He needed someone in his corner so badly, and Phillip was one of the few people he could trust. He stopped short. He was actually willing to trust a lawyer with his future. *Shit!*

"Yes!" Phillip looked desperate. "Please, you've got to believe me. We have to find a way to stop this ridiculous case from going to court tomorrow."

"Tomorrow?" Why did everything always have to happen right now? It was just like a bloody cake! Bake it to perfection…without any time for prep!

"Yeah, my boss insists." Phillip put his head in his hands. "Judge Sexby, the one who told me about your father being a former Fire Judge, isn't likely to grant another extension. There seems to be a lot of pressure from somewhere for this case to be handled quickly."

"So we've got to act quickly." Daine took a deep breath.

His thoughts still raced. His father had been a Fire Judge? Whatever that meant. He needed to come back to it, but there were more urgent decisions to be made right now. Like whether or not he was going to take this seriously. He frowned. Phillip was too agitated to be making this up. And it seemed he had done nothing but help Daine ever since they'd met. He might as well believe him.

"When exactly is this trial going to take place?" Daine hoped they'd have some time to prepare, find out some details.

"You believe me?" Phillip looked up, hope making his brown eyes shine.

"Yeah, you sound like you really mean it when you say you want to help me." He shrugged. "Anyway, you haven't done or said anything to make me suspicious."

"Oh, Daine, thank you." Phillip stood and took him into his arms. "That's such a relief. At least we can fight them together now."

Daine wanted Phillip's kiss, but this wasn't the time. Phillip had other ideas, though, his lips falling in a soft touch on Daine's mouth. It was gentle, so different from earlier. Phillip's tongue stroked his in slow, tender movements that made his heart speed up and his cock harden in anticipation. He almost cried when Phillip pulled back.

"What we need is a plan." Phillip kept his arms around him.

"Yeah, I can think of a few things. I need to find out what's really going on with my father and my uncle. Since I can't reach either of them, I'll have to try to find my grandmother. She'll probably know what went down."

"That's a great idea." Phillip's voice rumbled in his ear. "I can help you track her, if you want?"

"I might need the help. She lives in France now, that's all I know." He hadn't heard from her in years. He hoped she was still alive.

"I'll have to pretend to be going ahead with the case." Phillip sounded worried. "But you've got to believe me that whatever I say or do in an official capacity is only to stop anyone from being suspicious."

"I get that." Daine felt like this was a mixture of heaven and hell. "You know the old saying that the sins of the father visit themselves upon the son?"

Phillip nodded.

"That's me. I feel like all these sins that aren't mine just got dumped on me."

"I'm not going to let them hurt you," Phillip said.

Something in his eyes gave Daine pause.

He's not telling me everything. Shit. I'm really in trouble…and I have no idea why.

* * * *

In the small hours of the morning, Phillip stretched his tired muscles and growled at the empty coffee-maker in the corner of his office. He hadn't even bothered to go home. He knew sleep would only elude him and at least here he could pretend to be busy. With all these superpowers around, you'd think they'd come up with a way to keep it filled. But no, he still had to get up and do it himself.

He'd lost count of how many cups he'd had since he'd got here late last night. Dawn was beginning to creep over the horizon and he still wasn't much further than when he'd started. He absently scooped grounds into the filter and switched the machine on.

Returning to his desk to wait for the coffee to be ready, he looked over the ton of notes he'd made. Finding Daine a lawyer who would at least be competent hadn't been easy. He had a couple of names now, but getting them approved by the judge, who might have someone different in mind, would be a challenge. He also had to be careful not to appear to be too eager to find a good lawyer for Daine. Until he was sure which side his boss was on, he had to play his cards close to his chest.

The scent of fresh-brewed coffee wafted over, and he went to pour himself a new mug. Sipping the reassuring, hot liquid, he wandered over to the window to enjoy the sunrise as it painted the cityscape in soft colours.

His preparations for the case, his pseudo arguments and non-existent evidence were as ready as he could make them. He wasn't sure how anyone could think to make them stick, though. Any first-year law student would see there was no basis to prosecute.

Did Mr. Arden have something up his sleeve? Some last minute revelation? But then, why would he go through the motions of letting Phillip look for evidence? How much of this was a cover-up—and for what?

"You're in the office early." Mr. Arden's voice from right behind him almost made him jump. "Good, that gives me at least some confidence that you're finally taking this case seriously."

He turned around, trying to compose his face into a neutral expression before he had to face his boss.

"Good morning, sir." He walked back to his desk. "What can I do for you?"

"Just wanted to check whether you're ready for this afternoon, but it looks to me like you've got everything well in hand." Mr. Arden glanced across the messy desk. "Even if your organisation seems a bit chaotic."

God, he hoped the man wouldn't want to go over the facts. The case was wafer-thin, and the smallest amount of poking would make the holes more than obvious. Phillip was pretty sure the judge would see that the minute he'd finished presenting the case. If Mr. Arden saw it now, who knew what he might do? He might even be able to come up with something more solid. And where would that leave Daine?

"Shall we go over your plan of attack?" Mr. Arden took a seat and waved at the stacks of papers. "If you can find your way through all of this, that is."

"Certainly." Shit, he was in for it now.

But the presentation went better than he thought. Mr. Arden didn't interrupt him, and even started nodding about halfway through. He sat back when he was done, desperate for another coffee—possibly something stronger—but too afraid to move.

"Very good." Mr. Arden smiled. "I'm pleased with what you've managed to come up with. The evidence may be a bit thin on the ground, but your arguments are solid. It should be enough to get the case going."

Huh?

"I'll see you this afternoon." Mr. Arden got up and walked towards the door.

Something was definitely not right here.

"Don't be late," was Mr. Arden's parting shot before he left, on his way to his corner office down the corridor.

What the hell had just happened?

Phillip blinked a few times, deciding he needed more coffee. As shocked as he was by the lack of reprimands from his boss, he was going to fall asleep on his feet if he didn't get more caffeine into his system. He wasn't sure if he could make it to the trial without a nap.

Yet another mug in his hand, he returned to the window. Somewhere out there, his lover was trying to find the information they'd need to find out who was behind these false accusations.

He wished he'd heard from Daine by now. He'd found his grandmother's address and phone number earlier, but Daine hadn't wanted to call the old lady in the middle of her night. Since it was dawn here, it should be mid-afternoon in France. Had he been able to talk to her? What had he found out?

They desperately needed some sort of information that would lead them to the real culprits. Right now, it could be almost anyone. Without some sort of evidence, he wouldn't stand a chance of making a counter-suit stick. He checked the time. He'd fought calling Daine all night. This was a sticky situation, for both of them. He couldn't call a man he was supposed to prosecute and yet he badly wanted to hear the guy's voice. Damn it. He stared at the phone, willing it to ring. He found his jaw set, his back teeth grinding. What was Daine doing? Thinking?

Heck, why hadn't Daine called him?

Chapter Seven

"Thank you." Daine barely held back his frustration as he banged the receiver back into the phone cradle.

Well, that had been a stupid exercise in futility! He wanted to throw the phone at the wall, but it wouldn't do any good. All hope of locating his elusive parents was now out of the window.

His grandmother wasn't at the address and phone number Phillip had dug out for him late last night. Of course, the old lady didn't have a mobile, so trying to reach her on her *extended vacation*, as the butler had called it, was impossible. The fact that she had a butler almost made him laugh, but the situation was too serious for humour.

It was three a.m. He was dead on his feet and had no idea what to do next. Lacking any constructive ideas, he decided he'd better get a few hours' sleep. Thank God he'd arranged for Ernie to run the kitchen and for Lilly to open the bakery today. That way he didn't have to be there at his usual time, which was only an hour from now.

But Daine couldn't sleep. He was too wired. He lay in bed, staring at the ceiling. Where to begin? It started with his parents, of course. And his relationship with them was complicated. He smiled to himself. This seemed to be the new catchphrase everyone used these days, especially on the Internet. It was the description *du jour* whenever people had to fill in the space on Facebook for their relationship status.

It's complicated.

Yeah, it sure as hell was.

He could remember the last conversation he'd had with his parents. That part had *not* been complicated. They'd run out on him. His dad hadn't given him much of a reason, beyond needing to leave San Francisco. He wanted out of the business. Venezuela beckoned.

Anytime you want us, you think about us and you'll find us, he'd said.

How sad that his dad apparently thought Daine still believed in fairytales... *Hold on...* With what Phillip had told him about his dad having superpowers—maybe he'd actually believed it would work for Daine? But how could his dad have assumed Daine had any powers, without even a shred of evidence? That statement had either been wishful thinking on his father's part or a way to give Daine hope without having to fear he'd ever find and bother them.

Be that as it may, whether or not Daine had superpowers didn't matter in this context. If the statement had been meant to give him hope, it had definitely failed to do its job. After all, he'd never even thought about that conversation since...until this moment.

Daine stood and peered out the window.

"I sure need you now, Dad," he said to the city street below him. "I'm in deep trouble."

He turned away from the window and stumbled, falling squarely on his ass. More from the shock than the actual tremors, but still.

Earthquake!

He felt the rumble of the angry Earth at his feet. San Francisco had been bracing itself for a big one for some time, but this earthquake didn't feel all that serious. His entire building seemed to sway, but didn't collapse into a pile of rubble. That was the frightening aspect of the Earth shaking this way. A strong reminder that Mother Earth was more forceful than anything man-made.

When the seizure stopped, Daine took a breath. Nothing had fallen, thank God.

He turned to the phone. The urge to call Phillip and check on him was strong. No. He wouldn't act like a needy teenager. Phillip would be fine. Besides, Daine had bigger issues than a trembler to deal with. He turned away from the phone and sat up. His hands squelched.

Squelched?

Holy heck, he was sitting in mud! His heart stuttered. His mouth went dry.

His apartment was gone. He was sitting in the middle of a wet patch of soggy ground just outside of what appeared to be an outhouse. A man was sitting on the can, a roll of toilet paper at his Birkenstock-shod feet. He flipped the pages of a newspaper in his hands.

Daine's gaze narrowed.

The man glanced down at Daine, his eyes widening in shock.

Daine scooted up to his knees. His voice, when it finally worked, came out in a croak.

"Dad?"

* * * *

Phillip gripped the edge of his desk. The earthquake had been a small one, but having never experienced one before, it might have been massive for the effect it had on him. He trembled in his very shoes, several seconds after the actual shaking stopped. He checked the time. Seven a.m. He would forever remember the time and place of his first genuine California earthquake. His urge to pick up the phone and check on Daine was overwhelming. He reached over, but Declan was in his office now with papers for him to check.

"Any idea how strong that was?" Phillip asked.

"How strong what was?" Declan cocked a brow at him.

"The earthquake."

"We had an earthquake?" Declan's head tilted, as if he'd been asked a question that threw his body out of alignment.

"Yes, just now. You didn't feel it?"

"Um...no." Declan's gaze shifted from side to side. "Let me ask some of the others, just to make sure."

He left the office and Phillip swung his chair around to gaze at the view of downtown San Francisco. The sky was an unusual swirl of colours. Pink streaks infused the blue and white above. Did this usually happen after an Earthbound jolt? He missed Daine. He felt the man pulling away from him, like sand slipping through his fingers. He'd just shared the same earthquake, still shared the same air space and same patch of sky with Daine, but he felt so terribly far away from him.

"Sir?"

Phillip swung around again.

Declan stood in the doorway and lifted his hands in a helpless gesture. "No earthquake. I asked around and I even checked online...nothing. Sorry."

Phillip nodded. He felt totally stupid now. Perhaps he'd imagined it, and yet, the painting on his wall was slightly off and the sideboard containing his favourite dishes of candy must have moved. There were jelly beans scattered on its lacquered top.

Declan leaned over Phillip's desk with the papers in his hand.

"Thanks," Phillip said. "I'll look them over."

"Mr. Arden wants them signed immediately, if not sooner." Declan's tone of voice was grating on Phillip's nerves.

Phillip held out his hand for them, trying not to recoil when Declan's fingers unnecessarily brushed against his.

"Ah..." Phillip drew back from the unwanted contact.

"Anything wrong?" Declan asked. His gaze apparently took in the crooked picture, because his hand shot out to straighten it.

"That will be all, Declan, thank you." Phillip stood. He realised now that his assistant was harbouring some sort of deluded crush on him. Phillip wasn't the kind of guy who thought every man he met had a thing for him. But Declan's odd, bossy ways suddenly clicked into place, made some sort of weird sense. It alarmed Phillip because there was something about Declan that had never sat right with him.

"You okay?" his assistant asked.

"Sure. No problems."

"Should I wait for you to sign those papers?"

"No," Phillip said. "I have a small errand to run."

"But—"

Phillip cut him off. "I'll be back within the hour." *I think.*

"Where are you going?"

"I have to check on something."

Phillip was not about to tell Declan he was heading to Fabulous Cupcakes. He had a bad feeling something was wrong with Daine. He couldn't explain it, but he had to leave. He needed to check what was going on.

"I'll take these with me," Phillip said, snatching up the paperwork.

* * * *

Daine stared at his father. How the hell had he turned up here — wherever here was? Based on the trees surrounding them, the mud on the ground and the odd-looking outhouse, it was a fairly safe bet he wasn't in San Francisco anymore.

"Can't you give a man a little privacy?" His father reached to his left and slammed a rickety wooden door shut, flecks of mud landing on Daine's face.

He skidded back on his knees, his senses reeling, both from the stickiness of the mud and the shock of seeing his father after all this time.

Daine forced himself to his feet, the clay-like mud making things difficult. His father emerged, zipping up his jeans. He looked the same, maybe a little greyer at the temples. The familiar scowl seemed etched on his features for life.

"'Bout time you came to visit me. Still the same klutz, I see."

Now I know why I stayed away. Dad is such a charmer…

"We need to talk," Daine said, his feet skidding across the ground.

"Nice to see you, too," his father snapped.

He stalked past Daine.

"Dad, I'm on trial tomorrow in some weird-ass court I never even knew existed. I've been told I'm suspected of having all these alleged superpowers I never knew anything about." What would it take to get his dad to listen to him?

His father turned, a look of venom on his face. The spite in his angry gaze shocked Daine.

"There's nothing *alleged* about your superpowers, Daine. You inherited them from me, fair and square. And let me tell you, in my day, I was a force to be reckoned with." His father smirked.

He turned again and walked off, Daine trying to keep up with him.

"Why didn't you tell me about them? They're saying I abused my powers! Dad, until today I had no idea I even had any." Daine was ready to grab his father by the arm to make him stop walking away from him.

"Yeah? And?" His father kept walking.

"*And?*" Daine fought to keep his temper in check. "I'm in trouble!"

"And?"

Daine stopped moving, his feet sinking into the ground under his shoes.

"I need your help." Damn it, why did his father make things so difficult for him? Hell, he knew the man hadn't wanted to be found, but shouldn't the mention of his son going on trial for something he didn't do cause some sort of willingness to at least listen, if not help?

"Fantastic!" The old man wheeled around, throwing his hands in the air. "*Now* you need my help. You didn't need my help when you went against my wishes and changed college courses. You didn't need my help when you went against my wishes, yet *again*, and took over the bakery.

You should have let your uncle take it. You brought all this on yourself, kid."

He punched the air for emphasis.

His father's angry glare felt like a stinging slap. The old man turned and stalked off, leaving Daine stuck in the mud. Literally. As a kid, it had been one of his favourite games. As an adult, it blew monkey chunks. Struggling to lift his shoes out of the sucking morass, he hobbled after his father. The mud made his skin itch and his clothes felt wet and uncomfortably warm.

"Dad!"

"*Dad!*" His father whirled around and mimicked him, a sour expression of hatred on his face. "You're a waste of space, Daine. Your life..." His father stopped and put his hands on his hips. "You still queer, kid?"

Daine almost fell back on the ground. That's what all this was about? He'd forgotten the whipping he got from his father when he came out to his parents. His mother had been accepting, his father had been...homicidal.

"Where's Mom?" he asked, fighting the injustice of his father's inexplicable fury and his hateful words. *You're a waste of space...*

God, no wonder I blocked the bad memories and focussed on my work.

"You been having a good time enjoying your superpowers, queer boy?" his father jeered.

"Oh, yeah. Having tons of fun. I've been working like a friggin' dog for eighteen hours a day since you left. I've worked damned hard to make Fabulous Cupcakes a success, Dad. I wanted you to be proud." He'd thought the bakery had been his father's dream and making it successful would at least earn him some respect. It looked as though that had been a huge fucking miscalculation.

His father scoffed and walked away.

"Proud, my ass," he heard his father mutter.

"So, if that's me making the most of my superpowers, then yeah, I'm guilty as charged!" His voice was raw from the shouting and he was close to tears.

Fuck!

Daine's shouting seemed to set off a light rainfall. A bird flapped over his head. His father had vanished. Daine tried to follow him but got lost in a thick rainforest. He saw a gigantic tree python slither inches from his arm. He hated snakes. And spiders. The rain fell harder. How could his father just abandon him this way?

Shit! How the hell had his world just collapsed? He stood in the pelting rain, feeling hysteria creeping up on him. He was no closer to finding out who was behind the accusations that had been brought against him, and he was about to go on trial for these mysterious powers of his.

At least I know now that the powers are real. Phillip wasn't lying and he isn't crackers. Phillip...my God. He shut his eyes to the deafening sound of the rain. Then just as quickly as it had started, it stopped. Water still dripped from his head onto his body. He raised his face to a sliver of sunshine. How had he come here in the first place? Oh, yeah, he'd thought about his dad and the need to see him. He focussed on that.

A crackle of thunder and a spurt of heat followed. He felt as though he'd been flung by a huge, invisible force through time and space. He screamed when he saw the pile of mud waiting for him. He swerved and hit a hard patch of earth, landing at a pair of feet. Birkenstocks. He recognised them and glanced up from his father's feet.

His dad's mouth curled into a sneer. "Not bad, for an amateur."

Daine scrambled to his feet. Blood trickled down his nose.

"Don't spill blood everywhere, boy," his father said, walking up two stairs to a cabin-style house.

Daine followed. He wasn't going to be left behind anymore.

"Stay where you are!" his father commanded.

He reached behind the door and tossed Daine a towel that could have benefitted from a good wash. It was better than nothing, so Daine mopped his face, trying not to inhale the mildewed odour.

"Finesse, boy. You gotta learn finesse. You want to be someplace, see someone, you think about them. Focus. Keep your thoughts calm and you'll just show up. We're people of the Fire path, kid. Too much agitation and you end up looking like you do right now." His father gestured at him.

Daine looked down at himself. *Finesse*. His life was going to shit and his father suggested finesse.

"Thanks for the advice," he said, trying hard to keep his tone calm. He had no idea what had got into his father. They'd had some good times when he was a young child. Now Daine realised that, as he'd got older, his father had got more secretive.

"So, that's it, Dad? Finesse? That's all you gotta tell me?"

His father put a finger to his chin as if he pretended to consider the question.

"Pretty much."

"Thanks."

"Not a problem. Oh, and leave the towel. It's the only one I've got." His father smirked, as if that was some kind of joke.

Daine chucked it back at him. His father caught it, a strange look appearing on his face.

Man, he wants me out of here.

Daine turned, trying to keep his thoughts calm. He wanted to go home. Clearly, wanting to see his father had been a bad idea. Actually coming here to see him hadn't been his plan, and now that he had, it didn't look like the old man was going to help him any time soon, either. What was he still doing here? It was time to go back. Maybe Phillip had found a way to help him. Barring that, he was sure they were going to convict him.

He whirled around again, to say goodbye, and caught his father's hopeful expression. It ran from his face as soon as he noticed Daine looking. Well, that was odd. Or had he just been hoping that Daine would leave without another word?

"Why do you want me to go so badly?" Daine asked.

His father looked surprised. He seemed to be rifling through his Rolodex of bitter responses but settled for, "We've got nothing to discuss."

"I'm not leaving." Not before he got to the bottom of this.

"Jesus, don't you ever learn? I don't want you here. If they ever find out—" His father stopped, slapping a hand to his mouth.

Daine had never seen him so angry.

"Who's they?" This was the first hint of something useful.

His father's face turned white with rage.

"Don't you realise that by going against my authority you made things needlessly tough for yourself, kid? You think it's been easy, knowing all this time that you worked harder than most to make your dreams come true?"

"You always told me if I worked hard I'd reach my goals."

His father stared at him, shocked.

"I said that?" He stared at the ground. "I don't...I don't remember that."

"You never said anything about twitching my nose and all of a sudden life being peachy. I'm sure I would have remembered that." Daine was determined to find out exactly what his father thought he'd genetically passed on to Daine.

There was a movement in the house. He'd caught it only from the corner of his eye, but he was sure there was somebody watching them from one of the front windows. He turned his head to glance over and the slash of gaudy red fabric at the window moved.

Hah! Someone else was here in this wilderness.

"Is that Mom?" Daine asked. His voice trembled. For God's sake, why was his mother hiding?

"It's not her. Now, please, go." His father's lips were drawn into a tight line.

"What do you mean? Where is she?" Who else could it be?

The curtains moved again. Daine looked over and caught a man staring at him.

"Where is my mother?" Daine asked. "I'm not leaving until you answer me."

"She's not here," his father said.

"Yeah, so you say." Daine couldn't resist a little jab. "So, who's your boyfriend skulking around the window?"

His father blanched. "Who the fuck told you?"

"He really is your boyfriend?" Daine stared at his father. He'd thought he was joking. "You're *gay*?"

"Shit, Daine." His father sighed, looking resigned to his fate as his shoulders slumped. "I've spent half my life denying my natural urges and the other half making up for them."

"Oh, grow up, Marcel," a voice said from inside the house. A man came out, brushing right past his father.

"Christopher, stay out of this." His father looked really pissed off now, his hands fisted. Yep, the old man was angry.

Daine stared hard at the handsome young man with blond hair and blue eyes, who now approached him. Daine had seen the guy somewhere but couldn't place him.

"I'm your rude father's lover," Christopher said.

"And I'm his unwanted son." Daine grinned, liking Christopher already.

He shook Christopher's hand. The guy had a firm grip, always a good sign of a strong character.

"Where do I know you from?" Daine asked. "I know I've seen you someplace before."

"No, we've never met." Christopher took his arm. "Come and take a shower. Your father's being such an ass."

"But he said that was the only towel he had." Daine pointed to the one his father was still holding.

"He's just grumpy. He's been waiting for you to show up for quite a few years, you know." Christopher tugged at his arm until he started moving towards the house.

"Have not," his father muttered as they passed him.

Christopher led him to a bathroom and handed him a soft, fluffy towel.

"We live in a very delicate eco-balance here. You'll need to keep it short. Three minutes. I'll bang on the door if I don't hear the water stop." Christopher squeezed his arm. "He's really pleased to see you."

"Yeah, pleased like he got a case of the clap." Daine shook his head. If that was pleased, he definitely wanted to be out of here before his dad got mad.

"Honey, I fixed that." Christopher gave him a gentle little shove into the bathroom and closed the door on him.

Was the guy joking? When had his father ever had the clap?

Daine quickly stripped and stepped into the shower. A large lizard crawled up the wall. He ignored it. His skin felt like it was on fire. The lizard slipped through a crack in the wall, only a tiny portion of its tail visible. Daine grabbed a knobbly ball of soap and rubbed it on his skin. It didn't have much of a scent but he already felt better.

Oh, I wish I could see Phillip right now. I really miss him.

A second later, there he was, standing beside Phillip at the counter of Fabulous Cupcakes.

"Ah...I'd like to have a chocolate, salted caramel cupcake," Phillip was saying to the person behind the counter.

"We're out of those," the harried woman said. She peered over the counter. "Daine?"

The place was packed. Phillip's head whipped to the side.

"What are you doing here?" Phillip asked, eyes widening. "Naked?"

I gotta get back. Daine shut his eyes.

He found himself back in his father's bathroom, turning off the taps just as Christopher started hammering on the door.

"I've got some clean clothes for you, or do you want to nip home and get some?" Christopher's grin was audible through the door.

Daine stood rooted to the spot, totally bewildered. This superpower business was getting out of hand. Jumping from place to place like this, just on the basis of a thought, was distracting, not to mention dangerous. He had to find a way to get it under control. Why had it never happened before anyway? He'd wished to be elsewhere on occasion, but nothing had ever happened. He sighed. Yet another question his dad probably wouldn't want to answer.

"You okay in there?" Christopher asked.

Daine couldn't think straight. Never mind how he'd got there, the store had been packed even more than usual. Utter bedlam. He'd wanted to see Phillip and there he'd been. Who the hell had the woman at the counter been? Daine tried to place her.

"Sweetheart, are you okay?" Christopher opened the door and peered around the frame at him. "I know, it's all a bit shocking, isn't it?"

Daine looked at the man and slowly nodded.

"I'm going to lend you something to wear, you'll come out and have a cup of coffee, then we can have a nice talk." Christopher smiled.

It felt so good to have somebody making decisions for him that Daine just kept nodding. Christopher handed him a warn pair of running pants and a T-shirt.

"I think we're about the same size. Take your time." He closed the door again.

Daine took a deep breath. Christopher was sweet. He'd helped Daine calm down enough for him to place the woman as the student from Phillip's college who was helping out part-time. What the hell was her name again?

That wasn't a big problem, but the fact that the bakery looked to be in chaos was. Something else, too. Daine hastily dried himself off and got dressed.

Yes. He realised now. He'd appeared and disappeared, right in front of Phillip's eyes. Phillip would never believe now that Daine didn't have any superpowers he could have abused.

He'll throw the bloody book at me.

It would have been easy for Phillip to convince himself that it had been a figment of his imagination. That Daine hadn't appeared as if by magic, or rather, superpowers, and then vanished just as fast. Except for the puddle of water he'd left behind.

There was also the fact that a frazzled Lilly kept squawking, "Did you see that? Where'd he go?"

In a dramatic whisper, she leaned across the counter to Phillip, adding, "Am I delusional or was he buck naked?"

"Who?" Phillip asked, trying to divert the woman, hoping she'd realise how stupid she sounded and forget the whole thing. His gaze darted around the bakery. Who else had seen Daine? How much damage control was going to be needed?

"The naked man," a woman behind Phillip said. "He was staring at you."

"Me?" Phillip felt a tremor of pleasure, but kept his cool. "No, I didn't notice. I came here for the cupcakes. What else do you have available, Lilly?"

"Not much," she said. "We're in a bit of a muddle today."

His usually unflappable student looked stressed out.

"Daine normally runs such a tight ship, and is always on time and in control. But he didn't come in this morning. Cairo came and went and then somebody from Homeland Security showed up demanding to see the kitchen staff's green cards. They all had them except poor Ernie, on account of the fact he was robbed last night at gunpoint. Can you believe that? Right out the back alley. We've called Daine several times, but nobody's heard from him."

Phillip knew something was really wrong but had no clue how to fix it.

"Are you getting something or not?" the woman behind Phillip huffed.

"Not," he said. "Lilly, where's Ernie now?"

"They took him. They arrested him. And he's the head chef today." Lilly wrung her hands.

"I'll just pop into the kitchen and have a word with the crew," Phillip said.

"Will you?" Lilly said, as if that answered all her prayers. She pointed to the left and hurried over to open a half-door hatch in the counter. He went through to the back as the woman who was next in line complained about Phillip to Lilly.

The kitchen was more bedlam.

"What happened?" Phillip asked.

The staff members exchanged glances. Nobody said a word.

"Look, I'm a very good friend of Daine's. I came to help. Now, what's happened to Ernie?" It was as good a place as any to start investigating what was really going on.

One of the kitchen hands mopped the floor.

"Man," he said, "Ernie showed them the police report from last night. He got beat up real bad. He showed them the bruises on his face. And still they took him."

Phillip tried to absorb all this.

"What is your name?" he asked, trying to keep his tone gentle. It was clear the men were frightened.

"Antonio," came the whispered response.

Phillip nodded in what he hoped was an encouraging way. "Nobody's heard a word from Daine?"

"No." Another guy shook his head. "Cell phone is full." His evident emotion and thick Mexican accent tore at Phillip. This country had been built on the backs of hard-working immigrants, and he knew for a fact that Daine had secured work papers for his entire staff.

"No leave message." The guy turned sad eyes on Phillip.

"And Cairo?"

"She run," the guy said, imitating somebody taking off. "She no good, that one."

"What do you need?" Phillip asked, pulling out his phone.

"We need Daine." Antonio had stopped his mopping.

Don't we all?

"How many workers do you need?" Maybe throwing some more manpower at this would help reduce the chaos, enabling him to get a few answers.

"We no need workers," the guy beside him said. "We need food. No deliveries. Everybody scared to come here now."

"Who brings the supplies? Who does Daine order from?" Shit, this was a bigger mess than he'd thought.

The men looked at each other.

"We can tell 'im, Silvio," Antonio said.

"We can't tell him," another one said.

"Why can't you tell me?" Phillip felt himself losing his cool.

"Because he has pro'lems. We get new...truck. Now we don't know."

"You don't know?" Phillip couldn't believe his ears. What problems? What the hell was going on?

"Where are the books? Doesn't he keep orders someplace?" Paperwork was usually the answer, so he'd start there.

The men looked at each other.

"We have break-ins," Antonio said.

"Really?" Phillip was shocked. Daine had never said anything.

All the men nodded.

"Started last week. They take anything they see." Antonio shook his head.

"He move the books," Silvio added.

Upstairs. They had to be upstairs in the apartment.

"What exactly do you need in terms of deliveries?" Maybe he could figure out who to order from once he'd looked at the papers.

The men all looked at each other.

"Everything," Antonio said. "The people who broke in last night and beat up Ernie...they took a lot of stuff." He frowned. "Who steals flour? Weird, huh?"

Phillip ran out the back door and caught Cairo on her phone, cigarette in hand, pacing the alleyway.

"Cairo!"

She glanced at him, surprise in her eyes. She turned and ran. Phillip ran after her, but she'd vanished. He looked in both directions, but she was clearly gone and going to be of no use.

He returned to the bakery. He found the back entrance to Daine's apartment above the store. Using his credit card, he wedged the door open and went inside.

There was mud all over the floor and things were in disarray. Where the hell had the mud come from?

"Daine?" he called out.

His phone rang. He checked the readout. It was the bakery phone number.

"Hello?" he said, hoping it was Daine.

It was Lilly and she was hysterical.

"What did you say to the guys in the kitchen? They've all bolted. I'm here on my own with a shop full of hungry people!"

Chapter Eight

Daine walked into his father's kitchen and inhaled the smell of freshly baked bread. It made him feel a little better.

"I smell corn bread and sweet potato. Am I right?" he asked.

"Very good," Christopher said. "I've just baked Venezuelan *arepas* – it's a traditional corn pancake we make. I put some sweet potato and nutmeg purée in this batch. It's to die for."

Daine realised he was starving and snatched one of the round, pocket-shaped *arepas* from the colourful platter on the table.

He bit into it and almost swooned. The *arepas* was light, airy and deceptively easy to consume, leading the way to an urgent desire for more. He'd eaten three before he noticed the giddy smile on Christopher's face and the watchful expression on his father's.

"Where are we exactly?" Daine asked.

"Isla Margarita, or Margarita Island," his father said, looking sullen.

"It's one of the largest islands off the coast of Venezuela." Christopher glanced over his shoulder as he dropped more batter into a large, hot skillet.

"What brought you here, Dad?" Daine reached for another *arepas*.

"He did." His father pointed to his lover.

Christopher turned, an expression of mock horror on his face. "Marcel, now you *know* that's not true."

"I wanted to get away from everything. I came out and told your mom about Christopher."

"You thrashed me when I came out to you," Daine reminded him.

His father avoided the significant look Christopher shot in his direction.

"That's different," his father said, his cheeks bright red. "You were sixteen. I was in my forties."

"How's that different?" Christopher wanted to know.

"I wept after I did it and I did apologise," his father said.

Daine shrugged. "Your exact words were that it hurt you more than it hurt me. You'd never lied to me before that."

Christopher looked shocked. "You *said* that?"

"It was a long time ago." His father's voice rose. "I'm sorry, okay?"

The three men were silent.

"I think it was a reaction to my own deep-seated feelings about my sexuality. When I said it hurt me more than it hurt you, I was being an ass —"

"Yeah, you were," Christopher said. "You beat your son!"

"I'm over it," Daine said. "Sort of."

His father looked at him. "How much do you know about the Secret Council?"

"Nothing." Daine needed to do something with his hands. He had to fight the urge to fling hot *arepas* at his father. He picked up the coffee cup beside him and poured a little milk from the jug on the table. He sipped. It was just the way he liked it. "I know you were a Fire Judge and something went wrong."

Christopher handed him a fresh *arepas*.

"This one has chocolate in it. It's my favourite." Christopher grinned.

Daine bit into it. It was melty and heavenly. He immediately began to wonder how he could duplicate this combination of textures and flavours in a cupcake.

"It was your destiny to be a Fire Judge, too," his father said.

Daine stopped eating. The *arepas* sat in his mouth like a rock.

"Swallow," his father said.

Daine swallowed.

"In the world of the elemental superpowers, the Secret Council is the body that is in charge of keeping law and order amongst people with superpowers. There are four Branch Councils that make the laws, each representing the natural elements; fire, water, air and earth. There is also the Superpower Court that upholds the laws made by the Branch Councils. It is also divided into four parts representing the natural elements. The Paradis family are Fire People and we are supposed to hold regular workaday jobs, plus we have our work for the Fire Court. You and I come from a long line of Fire-Power workers. I was supposed to train you, prepare you to replace me one day as a Fire Court judge."

Daine stared at his father, mesmerised. "So what happened?"

His father shrugged. "I was supposed to adjudicate on Christopher's trial. It was a big one. He faced violations charges and instead…we fell in love."

"Violations? Of what?" Daine couldn't help eating the *arepas*. They were so addictive.

"Food. He created a love potion and, well…the Superpower Court still won't approve it. But imagine if we could smuggle that stuff to all the countries of the world and a few drops went into the food supply everywhere? Everybody would be so blissed-out, there'd be no wars, no famine. Only love."

"That sounds…amazing." Daine couldn't see the downside of such a potion.

His father seemed to read his thoughts.

"The drug companies in the natural world and the Branch Councils in the superpower world all went mad. They depend on trouble and strife. If everybody's happy, there's no need for pills, for laws, nor for courts and lawyers…or Fire Judges. We could have made history and I guess in a way we did. I agreed to disappear. I gave up the right to my legacy. Your mom left for England and I hear she's happy with her new husband."

"She remarried?" Daine stopped eating again.

"Yes, Daine. She remarried." His father looked truly happy about that.

"You talk to her?" Daine was dizzy from all the revelations.

"Sometimes. Look, she's not happy that both her husband and son are gay. I guess these weren't Hallmark moments for her. She was even less happy about my superpowers." His father's cheeks coloured again. "I didn't tell her until I revealed my sexuality to her."

"She never knew?" Daine sat back. That probably explained why he was never even aware of his own superpowers. His father couldn't very well have taught him without his mom noticing that something unusual was going on.

"No." His father shook his head. "It was easier that way, both for me and for you. I wasn't sure you'd even inherited any superpowers until you were in your teens. You were a very late developer."

"Gee, thanks." Daine frowned. "So if you never taught me anything, what activated them now? I mean, when I made myself appear here a few hours ago?"

"It must have been the extreme emotional stress you were under." Christopher tilted his head. "It has happened before."

"It has?" At least he wasn't a total freak. "So, how do I control them?"

"Focus, kid, like I told you." His father looked impatient again.

"Look, I'm sorry, Dad, but that's less than helpful." Daine shook his head.

"The boy's right, Marcel." Christopher nodded, shooting an angry glance at his lover before he turned back to Daine. "Usually the powers develop slowly and children learn to deal with them as they grow up. When they are activated, as you called it, later in life, it takes patience to learn to deal with them."

"Not helpful" Daine almost growled. Why were they speaking in riddles?

"I know." Christopher chuckled, stopping when he saw Daine's anger. "The best you can do for now is to remember that any wish for, say, relocation that is extremely emotional or urgent will likely set them off. Staying calm and relaxed is your best strategy."

Yeah, right, like that was going to be easy with a trial coming up. Daine decided there wasn't anything more he'd be able to learn about controlling his abilities right now.

"So, what happened after you gave up the right to your legacy, as you put it?" Daine was at least going to find out what had happened with his father.

"I agreed to be stripped of my powers and my duties on the bench, and Christopher and I came here."

"What about the potion?" Daine wondered if this trial had anything to do with the establishment being worried about what had happened to it.

"We still have the recipe but we haven't made the stuff for years." His father glanced at Christopher, then back at Daine. "I had to swear not to tell you anything. And I didn't. You've never known about your birthright. Now, I don't know how I can help." His father looked worried.

Daine shrugged. He wished he had more coffee. Christopher bustled over with the pot and poured him a cup. Daine had so many questions.

"You left me, Dad. Didn't you miss me?"

"Did you miss me?"

"Yes and no."

His father laughed. "Same here, kid. I knew if you turned up it would be because you were in trouble." He gazed out of the window. "This is a dry island with hidden pockets. We picked the most remote place in the middle of a bloody forest and still you showed up."

"Sorry," Daine said.

One more *arepas* and a cup of coffee and he'd be on his way.

"Your father is a lying ass," Christopher said. "He's missed you like crazy. He talks about you all the time."

"Shut up, Chris," his Dad snapped.

"I won't shut up, Marcel. It's true. We have to help him. Now is not the time to live in secrecy and fear. There are monsters among us. We have to help Daine."

"We can't." His father was pale.

For the first time, Daine realised his father was petrified.

Christopher sat beside his father. There was a forthright, resolute warmth to Christopher that Daine couldn't help admiring, even as he struggled to absorb the truth of his place in his father's life.

He watched the way Christopher took his father's hand in his and rubbed his thumb against his father's fingers.

When he spoke, Christopher's voice was soft.

"He worried about leaving you. He worried you wouldn't find us. To make it easier to find us and so he'd feel a little bit closer to you, we moved here. Guess what we named this bay?"

Daine shook his head. "No idea."

"San Francisco." His father grinned.

He didn't know what to say. It was a lot to take on board in a short amount of time.

Christopher leaned closer across the table. "Daine, how did you find out about the trial? What led to it?"

"I met someone…for the first time in a long time. His name is Phillip Sedgwick and I thought he was a college professor. That part turned out to be true, but he just told me he came to the bakery to check me out…investigate is the word he used, actually." God, he wanted Phillip to be here.

"Sedgwick, you say?" Marcel's eyes flickered with interest.

Daine nodded.

"He's an attorney for the Fire Court?"

"That's what he told me. I thought he was nuts at first, but lately everything's been going wrong for me." Daine swallowed, feeling overwhelmed.

His father seemed lost in thought.

"His family, if it's the Sedgwicks I'm thinking of, they are a good, solid, Fire-Powers family. I started as a prosecuting attorney, you know." His father smiled.

"No, I didn't know." Daine almost rolled his eyes.

"Well, my problems started when I was elevated to the judicial bench. I knew Christopher through the bakery."

"You did?" Daine was intrigued to hear this.

"He was our best baker. He came to work with us and hadn't been there long when we realised—"

"We were in love," Christopher said.

"I had no idea." Daine tried to compute all of this.

"You were away at school. Listen, it's old news, except for the fact that, once I was on the bench, I felt the attempts at sabotage." His father frowned.

"There's something you're not telling me," Daine said. "What is it?"

His father turned evasive, but Christopher would have none of it.

"They've spent the last twelve months trying to figure out how to get him back on the council." Christopher grinned.

Daine stared at them, stunned.

"So...what? Coming after me is an attempt to persuade you to come back to work?" It would explain a lot.

Christopher and his father exchanged glances.

"Could be. Whatever you think about your father, they know he loves you. He did what he did to protect you." Christopher smiled reassuringly.

"I never thought they'd come after you," his father said. "I didn't think they'd stoop this low."

"So will you help me?" Daine asked.

His father shook his head. "I can't. The public humiliation. You have no idea. It was awful."

Daine slumped in his seat. "I guess I should go then." He tried to assemble his thoughts. "Know any good Fire Court attorneys?"

* * * *

Phillip hated going through Daine's personal papers, but he had no choice if he wanted to help fix the issues that were stopping the bakery from functioning. In the kitchen of the small apartment, he found boxes with well-kept files containing recipes, many with adjustments made for volume and taste. He found himself feeling sentimental when he noted Daine's little pencilled comments. He also found document files containing order sheets and invoices. He couldn't help feeling relieved that the guy did everything in a legitimate way. He didn't conjure up his ingredients, even if he had just materialised naked beside him downstairs.

Give him the benefit of the doubt. Let him explain.

Further reading showed that, in the last few weeks, Daine had experienced some inexplicable problems. Food deliveries had failed to show up but he'd been billed for them. Phillip bristled when he saw the correspondence between Daine and one of his vendors who threatened legal action despite the fact it was clear the vendor had not delivered the goods. Daine had switched companies and things seemed fine until the last two shipments failed to arrive.

Phillip detected an aggressive pattern of sabotage.

He lowered the piece of paper in his hand. He felt haunted by Daine's sweet smile and melting kisses. He'd never let on that he was dealing with such stress. Phillip felt enraged on his new lover's behalf.

What was this case really about, then? It clearly wasn't abuse of superpowers. He tried to remember the surprisingly small file of research Declan had finally presented him with yesterday, after he'd asked his assistant for the third time to give him answers to some of the specific questions he'd asked. One of them had been to find out why Daine's father had vanished so suddenly.

The file had said something about a love potion. *Huh.* He'd dismissed it at the time, thinking that it must have been an error. Now he wasn't so sure. It would explain why everyone was up in arms. If it existed, they were probably trying to either get control of the potion, or to make sure it was never used. If Daine's father had been involved, maybe he'd passed on the secret recipe to his son?

Time to find out.

He opened the cupboards and found an amazing selection of foreign spices. He felt vaguely disloyal opening exotic-looking containers with labels like Grains of Paradise. He sniffed the brown seeds and detected a strong, peppery smell. He opened the jar of pure maple grains, surprised at how the smell of maple syrup infused the dry contents. Sumac, galangale, nigella, mahlab—that one had a delicious scent of marzipan—the unusual names went on and on. Devil's Dung. Wow. What in the hell was that? The jar had been shipped from a gourmet condiment store. He opened it and turned up his nose. It was onions and garlic. He reopened the mahlab to get back the warm, comforting smell of almonds.

Phillip put everything back. He felt sheer relief not to have detected a single whiff of love potion. Daine was a man who cooked with some amazing ingredients, but it didn't look like love potion was part of his success.

Maybe someone else was to blame and was trying to divert attention from themselves by setting up Daine?

He longed to call Declan and ask him to research any recent cases of love potion violations but some inner intuition told him not to. He didn't trust the guy. It was a terrible way to feel, but it was true. He chewed his lip. There was one person in the office he trusted. Tokio Jones. She was a smart young woman who, if he was honest about it, could run rings around some of the attorneys in the law firm of Arden, Bainbridge, Chinook and Damek.

Phillip scrolled through the numbers on his phone. He was surprised to see Tokio's direct number was missing. He immediately suspected sabotage but couldn't understand why that specific number would be gone. He shook his head. He was overreacting because of what was happening to Daine.

He put a call through to the main switchboard at the office. The operator who took his call put him through to Tokio, whose careful, modulated tones comforted him. There was something about Tokio he just trusted.

"I want you to help me," he said.

"For you, anything." He could hear the smile in her voice. He pictured her short blonde hair, coffee-coloured skin and dazzling grin.

"This is strictly between us, Tokio. I want you to research any possible cases in the last few years of love potion violations. It's important. I need it urgently. I don't want you to talk to anyone but me. You have my cell phone number?"

"Of course," she said, "But is this related to the Paradis case?"

"How did you know?"

"I sent Declan a bunch of research on it days ago." Tokio sounded hurt.

"You did?" Phillip was definitely going to look for a new assistant. Declan had gone too far now. "I never saw any of that."

"I was desperate to be part of your team. Marcel Paradis lost his position as a peer of the court over a love potion case."

Phillip felt the fury mounting in him. So *that* was the missing connection. Why hadn't Declan told him the details? Why had he not told Phillip that Tokio wanted to be a part of his team? She was a tiger...a tiger who apparently wanted to claw Daine, but still, a job had to be done.

"He never told me and, as of this moment, you are a part of my team. I need you to tell me everything you know." Phillip might stand a chance now.

She began to rattle off information.

His phone rang. He checked the readout. The bakery number flashed. He put Tokio on hold to take the call.

"What's going on?" Lilly sounded unglued.

"I'll be right down," he said, snatching the latest invoice from the file and letting himself out of the apartment. Switching back over to Tokio, Phillip listened in increasing awe as she sketched out her findings.

For a moment he paused. He could smell the scent of his lover's skin. Daine always smelt like cupcakes and, inexplicably, fresh figs.

He shook his head. He descended the stairs as Tokio went on.

* * * *

"We can't help you get a defence counsel," his father said.

Daine hated seeing the fear in his father's eyes. The father he knew and loved had never seemed so cowed by life. It broke Daine's heart in a million places. He noticed the meaningful looks exchanged by the two men opposite him. He sensed that Christopher wanted to help, but wouldn't go against his life partner. Daine wanted to run, but also needed help. He had nowhere else to go. He'd just been pissed on from a great height by this whole superpower world. He tried not to feel bitter about that or the fact that his new lover, Phillip, was mounting a campaign against him.

"Christopher, I take it you are of the Fire House, too?" Maybe Christopher would help.

"Of course," his father snapped. "He wouldn't have been on trial in my court otherwise."

"Marcel, don't be a dick." Christopher looked at Daine. Flickers of pain in his eyes reminded Daine of the times he'd opened his oven door and seen that a cake had burned or maybe had fallen flat.

"Yes. I'm a Fire guy. I was open about the love potion. I was a...chemist..." Christopher looked lost all of a sudden.

"Sweetheart," his father said, "You can't call me a dick, then lie to my son."

Christopher's cheeks reddened. "I'm not lying."

His father heaved a sigh. "You gave up so much..."

"I didn't give up much." Christopher glanced at Daine. "Your father gave up everything for me. I always tell him he's like King Edward VIII to my Wallis Simpson."

Daine stared at him. Of course, he knew that the former British king abdicated his throne to marry the divorced woman of his dreams, but still, reference to a seventy-year-plus-old incident, though historically significant, got him thinking.

"Why are you staring at me?" Christopher asked.

"Who are you?" Daine asked. "I mean…what are you?"

Christopher's face lit up. "See, I told you he was smart. He can take it."

"He's a Magus," his father said, flicking a glance that spoke of love and awe towards his lover.

"A Magus?" Daine tried to absorb this. "You mean…some kind of magician?"

"No, magic has nothing to do with this." His father shook his head. "A Magus is like a high priest."

Christopher looked embarrassed.

"There are only five of them belonging to each elemental house throughout the world," Marcel said. "One of the Fire House ones, the Mage of Berwick, is a juror. He's a fair man, unless you date him. Don't flirt with him. He's dangerous."

"Flirt with him? I'm on trial for my life here," Daine spat out.

"Two others belong to the Fire Court system. Now that Christopher has walked away, it puts some pressure on his successor." His father looked pained, probably worried that he'd caused all this.

"Yeah? And who's that? Maybe he can help me," Daine said.

They stared at him.

"What?" he asked. Then it became apparent.

"Wait…you're not suggesting *I'm* a Magus?"

"Hello, nurse. He finally gets it," Christopher said.

A Magus. Me?

"Baking was my passion," Christopher said. "To avoid the death penalty, I agreed to no longer doing my healing work." For a moment, he looked devastated. His father reached across and gripped his hand.

"I think this trial is more to see if you're ready to step up to the plate and if you've been behaving ethically," his father said. "That's why I never contacted you once. Nobody can say you're tainted goods. At least you weren't until you showed up here."

Dang.

"What do I do now?"

"You go back," his father shouted.

"Darling, be reasonable. He needs a game plan." Christopher patted his father's hand in an obvious attempt to calm him down.

"Yeah, a game plan and some Valium would be swell." Daine was shaking.

His father shook his head. "I can't help you there."

Silence fell for a moment.

Daine couldn't help asking Christopher if he missed the superpower in his life.

Christopher's voice cracked when he said, "I still get to cook, but I've waited so long to talk shop with you."

His father grumbled, "Don't listen to me. I'm just your husband."

"You're so dramatic." Christopher nudged him. "Come on, let's show Daine the garden."

Daine wandered the rainforest property with them. He was impressed by the kitchen garden Christopher had cultivated. The two men walked through rows of herb plants, admiring things he normally had shipped to him from catalogues and online companies.

"I own a small café on the beach," Christopher said. "I love feeding people. It's tiny, and being where we are, we're off the radar, but I miss being able to help people, to cook for crowds."

He glanced at Daine's father, who sat in a deckchair in the middle of a ring of wild lavender, reading a dog-eared copy of *The Odyssey*.

"Your father likes the quiet life. He's pretty much retired now. Not just from the bench...from everything."

"No, I'm not, I'm the official food tester." His father grinned. Daine watched the way the two men bantered, the smiles, touches...man, his father was gay! It was still a shock.

"You're seeing Phillip?" Christopher asked, sounding almost shy.

"Yes. The trial attorney I face...I guess it's what, this afternoon?"

"Love will find its way," Christopher said.

"Yeah? Well, I wish he would find his way right here. If he stood right here in front of me, I'd give him a piece of my mind." Daine grinned. Hadn't his father said something about focus and emotional intensity?

* * * *

Phillip put a sign on both bakery doors, front and back saying, *Due to a family emergency, we are closed until tomorrow.*

"We really have no choice," Lilly said.

"No." Phillip agreed. He felt terrible, but, since the phone numbers on the invoice for Daine's deliveries were both disconnected and there was no kitchen staff, he really did have no choice.

"Don't you think something weird is going on?" Lilly asked. "I mean, I think it's weird."

Phillip tried not to jump to conclusions. He'd found Daine's keys and wallet in his apartment's kitchen. Where would he have gone without these essentials?

"Yeah…a little weird."

Outside the kitchen door, he checked it was locked.

"You know, it feels almost supernatural," Lilly said. "Some of the people who came in to the shop today were weirdoes. I mean, people in monk's robes, for Lord's sake…and they seemed really nosy. One of them asked me if the sesame seed cookies contained eye of pigeon and he seemed really disappointed when I said no."

Holy shit! The jury's here already and of course…the usual gallery watchers who love a Fire trial. They're already in town and they couldn't wait to come check it all out.

He couldn't help the stab of disappointment in his chest. Of all the days for them to come, when poor Daine's cooking was non-existent and the place was not up to par.

The signs on the doors weren't lying. Without Daine and his magic — *no, don't even think that word!* — touch, Fabulous Cupcakes weren't fabulous. Not by a long shot.

"Don't you think it's eerie? Like something weird is going to happen?" Lilly stared up at the sky. "Like a bad storm coming? Or an earthquake?"

The earth rumbled. They both lurched in different directions. He fell to his knees and heard a gasp. He looked down.

What the fuck? *Mud?*

"Phillip."

He turned, his knees slipping on the ground. He stared at the three men gazing down at him.

"Who…?" His addled gaze travelled to Daine, who grinned.

"What the fuck?" he asked Daine.

"This is my father," Daine pointed at an older version of himself. "The other one is his lover, Christopher—"

"His…lover?" Phillip's jaw dropped.

"And you know what the hell I am, right?" Daine's eyebrows rose.

Phillip struggled to his feet.

"Do you know what you put me through, disappearing like that? I don't know whether to kick your ass or kiss you," Phillip said.

"Hmm...I'm kinda torn myself." Daine leaned in and kissed him.

Phillip kept staring at Christopher. "You are who I think you are, aren't you?"

Christopher put his head to one side. "Who do you think I am?"

"Christopher Fire."

"That's me." Christopher nodded

Phillip kept staring at the three men. This was too strange for words.

"Fire? Your name is actually Fire?" Daine asked.

"Of course it is." Christopher looked indignant. "My family was born to that name."

"So you're the prosecuting attorney." Daine's father looked Phillip up and down. "You have an uncle called Jakob, do you not?"

"You know Uncle Jakob?" Phillip was ready to scream.

"We used to play golf together." Daine's father grinned.

"Come on, darling, we should leave them alone together. They have a lot to talk about." Christopher grabbed Daine's father and pulled him towards the house.

"We can't leave them alone. What if the council finds out they've been discussing the case?" Daine's father frowned.

"God you are...obtuse! Can't you see the mutual lust?" Christopher pulled harder, but Daine's father wasn't moving.

"No," his father said. "I'm constipated."

The others laughed.

"Oh, my God," Christopher muttered and finally dragged Daine's father away.

Phillip looked down at his ruined clothes.

Daine touched his arm.

"I'm sorry. I'm new at this conjuring thing. I only discovered it when I arrived here and landed in the mud, just like you. Phillip, you're here." Daine's smile made everything better.

"Yeah. Guess I am." As much as he wanted another kiss — and more — he couldn't be here.

"I've missed you," Daine said.

"Damn it. So have I. Are you okay?" In spite of himself, Phillip reached for him. "God, you've been through hell, and I'm so sorry."

Daine leaned closer to him, their lips meeting in a searing kiss.

"I don't think we should be doing this," Phillip said. It almost killed him to pull away from Daine. His mouth, the same one that just couldn't keep its two parts from any part of Daine's body, said words it — and the rest of his body — belied.

"Why? You don't want me anymore?" Daine asked.

"Want you? Of course I want you. It's just that I'm about to try you in a court of superpower law and —" Phillip knew it was the right thing to say, but he was amazed at how stupid that sounded in the face of his growing feelings for Daine.

"That didn't stop you before today." Daine shook his head, looking sad.

"I didn't...couldn't help myself. I can't think straight when you're around. It's hard to think about anything else — well, except maybe cupcakes — when I'm with you." It sounded like an excuse and he knew it, but it was the truth.

"Hmm...well, I don't see the problem. I'm the accused, you're the prosecuting counsel. I don't think a bit of slap and tickle should sway you one way or the other." Daine grinned.

"Slap and tickle?" What was Daine referring to?

"What would you rather have me say? A fuck and a feel?" Daine's grin turned impish.

Phillip stared at him.

Daine, the bastard, had started running his hand along Phillip's fly, his fingers working on the shaft itching for release.

"I stayed awake all night thinking about this." Daine's gaze was riveted to his crotch.

"Daine...no...I want this too, but we should wait."

"Wait?" Daine took his hand away. "You're right."

Chapter Nine

Daine moved away, just out of reach. The bastard!

Phillip lunged for him and fell face down into the mud. His head seemed stuck and panic set in when he found he couldn't breathe. He finally got free, gasping for air. For a moment, his wounded pride got the better of him, and he was determined to get back to his office and change.

Daine reached in and flipped him over.

"Make sure you tell the powers that be that I turned you over myself. No superpowers involved." Daine looked angry.

Phillip spluttered.

Daine came over to him, bending down. "I have you at a distinct disadvantage."

"Daine, help me up."

"No can do." He plopped into the mud, sinking to his knees and began unzipping Phillip's fly.

"What the fuck are you doing? Are you crazy?"

"Just a bit."

Daine pulled down Phillip's pants. The only pieces of clean skin on him were his cock and balls.

Phillip held his breath as his cock bounced in Daine's handsome face. Daine stared at it with hot lust.

Suck it. Lick it. Fuck. Touch me. Please. Touch it.

Phillip felt his ass reaching from the mud, yearning for closer contact with Daine, whose lips began stroking the head of Phillip's cock. Phillip began to breathe again. He was afraid of saying anything that would make Daine stop. Daine's chin rubbed against the shaft, as if he enjoyed the sensation of Phillip's cock against his face. Then, Lord have mercy, his tongue dipped out of his mouth then licked the head of Phillip's cock.

Yes!

He sucked Phillip all the way into his mouth, his fingers coming to Phillip's balls now. Phillip writhed underneath him.

Daine released him, making Phillip cry out in protest.

"No!"

Daine stood, shucking his running pants. He straddled Phillip's body, holding his cock against his own hard shaft. He bore down on Phillip's balls as he wriggled around on Phillip's lap. Phillip held Daine's hips steady. Their gazes locked.

"Hi," Phillip said.

"Hello, you. I've got a question."

Phillip lay back in the stupid grey stuff and cocked a brow.

"Clearly, we have no condoms and I'm wondering, as superpower carriers, are we immune from disease?"

Phillip laughed. "No, baby. We're not invincible. We're still like regular people, but we have a few extra-sensory powers."

"You know, I'm thinking that, pretty much, this superpower stuff sucks. You can go on trial at the drop of a hat. You can't abuse your powers... This whole thing blows monkey chunks." Daine was going to pout any second now.

Phillip grinned up at him. "Not completely. There's still a lot of wiggle room. And speaking of which, you have me in a bind here."

"I do, don't I?" Daine began to rock back and forth, sliding up and down Phillip's slick, wet thighs. He let go of Phillip's cock, letting his ass cheeks nestle the rigid length between them.

"Oh, God, that feels good." Phillip grabbed Daine's cock, the two men working against one another, hard friction, in perfect rhythm. Phillip erupted, his pleasure igniting Daine's sexual response. He came hard, with Phillip's fingers curling over the end of Daine's cock, coaxing him to a tremendous rush of peace.

Daine slumped on top of him. When he lifted his head and spoke, his words made Phillip smile.

"The defence rests."

* * * *

Back at the house, they showered and changed, the old man fuming on the other side of the door about short showers and spiritual wrath.

"No more than three minutes," he kept yelling.

"Shhh," Christopher would say immediately afterwards.

Phillip dried himself off, watching Daine step into a fresh pair of jeans that must have been borrowed, looking hotter than hell. Phillip picked up the pair Christopher had left for him, with an aged Abercrombie and Fitch shirt. It had a faint blue stripe through it. The shirt felt soft and good.

"How do we get back?" Phillip asked.

"Don't you know? Not that I'm sure I can do it again," Daine responded, doing up the buttons of a pale blue shirt.

Phillip shook his head. "I came here on your Fire thread, not my own."

Daine shook his head. "I have no idea what that even means."

"Hmmm…a superpower virgin. I love it. I'm gonna have so much fun teaching you." He took Daine's chin in his hand and kissed him.

"You two almost done in there?" Daine's father shouted.

"Yes," they shouted back.

Daine put his hand on Phillip's arm. "Can I ask you something?"

Phillip shrugged. "Sure."

"This Fire thread, did you use it to turn up outside the bakery the first night we met?"

"No, but I've used it at times…I'm frugal with it. I find it quite tiring. You create earthquakes. And you seem to have a fondness for mud." Phillip mock-frowned.

"Sorry."

"Don't be. But it might take some getting used to."

"You talk like we might have a future."

"I certainly hope so, Daine. I don't think you've been lying to me. I see no misuse of power. Not on your part anyway, but somebody sure as hell has been trying to submarine you. Why the hell didn't you tell me about the shipment problems and the break-ins?" Phillip was still mad about that.

"Well, it wasn't exactly pillow talk, was it?"

"No." Phillip stroked his lover's hair away from his cheek. "I have to go. The jurors are already assembled. I have to get to the court."

"I'm scared." Daine was paler than usual and his hands shook.

Phillip kept his hand on Daine's cheek. "I know you are. Look, I haven't had time to prepare you, but just tell the truth. Be yourself. You'll be fine. The court is intimidating, but I won't let them hurt you. I won't let them railroad you. I promise you that."

"I've worked so hard. I didn't cheat anyone or anything. Not even my taxes." Daine's eyes reflected pure emotion.

"I know, sweetheart." Phillip's heart broke at the anguish visible in his lover's face.

"If...if the impossible happens, and I'm found guilty, what's the worst that could happen to me?"

"Death, but it's not going to happen." Phillip would find a way to stop that if it killed him.

"*Death?*" Daine's eyes were huge.

"It's a violations of superpower charge and, because of your father, there's a lot of interest in this case." Not that this impressed Phillip in the least.

"Oh, swell. This gives a whole new meaning to the expression *a cake to die for*." Daine collapsed, Phillip managing to hold him up.

"It's not going to come to that." Phillip winced. "Nobody's been sentenced to death for...aeons."

"*Aeons?*" Daine's eyes were going to fall out of his head if he wasn't careful.

"Look, the worst that could happen is that you could be forced to close the bakery."

"But it's my life."

"I know. I promised I won't let them hurt you." Phillip would keep that promise no matter what.

"But you can't promise they won't shut me down."

Phillip hesitated. "I can promise you I will do my worst as a prosecuting attorney. They already know my case. I don't have a strong one against you."

"That's good...right?"

"Judge Sexby is a fair man...but I don't know, Daine. It's smoke and mirrors. Just when I think I've figured out who's behind the madness being brought down on you, I hit a dead end I will fight for you. You're a good man."

"So are you." Daine smiled.

Phillip felt better, even if it was totally irrational to let a smile affect him like that. He couldn't help himself, though.

They walked into the kitchen. Daine's father and Christopher stopped talking.

"We can't come with you," the older Paradis said.

"Of course we're going with him. He needs character witnesses. He needs his family. Who else can stand up for him? If he didn't get help from us to violate their freakin' superpowers, who else would do it? He knew nothing about them," Christopher insisted.

"No. We can't." Daine's father trembled with fear.

"They're going to point fingers at us," Christopher warned. "It will look bad if we're not there."

Daine looked miserable.

"It's okay, I understand," he said.

"No. We'll be there." Christopher sounded confident and somehow reassuring. "I'm so glad to finally know you." He moved over to Daine and hugged him.

"Thank you." Poor Daine seemed to cling to him.

"Son," Daine's father said, "You have to remember something. Appearances are deceiving. Not everyone who appears to be your enemy *is* your enemy. And not everyone who seems to be a friend is one. Remember that."

"Oh, for God's sake, darling, tell the man the truth. Tell him what you're talking about." Christopher rolled his eyes.

"I can't! You know I can't." Marcel's head lifted. He looked spooked. "Do you hear music?"

"Holy shit," Phillip said. "The trial's starting, and I'm in jeans and an old shirt."

"Forget that!" Daine's voice pitched to a quivering note of hysteria. "I don't have a defence attorney." He turned to his father. "Dad, help me!"

"I can't," his father said.

"Dad!"

The music grew louder, giddy, maddening, merry-go-round music. Phillip felt the world tumbling away from him. He felt gigantic hands pulling at him.

"We'll be there," Christopher shouted.

"Daine!" Phillip yelled. "Daine!"

Then the world went dark. He landed with a painful thud in a dark tunnel. He heard his own shallow, agonised breath. Feeling petrified and claustrophobic, he inched along what appeared to be damp walls. In some places the walls felt warm; in others, burning hot. He felt flames and the fear licked at him in all the wrong places.

As he neared a point of light in the distance, Phillip heard a deafening rumble. The roar of a crowd, as if they screamed for blood. Daine's blood.

"Order! Order!" an even more authoritative voice boomed over the rabble.

"The trial of Daine Paradis is about to begin!"

Another roar went up. Man, were they selling hot dogs and peanuts at this gig?

Phillip felt something prodding him from behind and the brush of fur against his skin. He had the peculiar sensation of being a Christian about to be fed to the lions.

* * * *

Judge Sexby stared down at Phillip, who found himself transported to his table on the prosecution's side, gripping the edges for support.

"What the hell is this? Casual Friday?" Judge Sexby thundered.

"Er...no, Your Honour." Phillip refused to look away.

"Care to explain yourself?" Judge Sexby's eyes narrowed.

No, I don't. "An unavoidable occurrence, Your Honour. In the course of pursuing new evidence in this case in—"

"A mosh pit?" the judge asked, giving him a steely stare.

The titter in the courtroom bugged Phillip. He hated being laughed at. It brought back horrible memories of school.

He raised his voice over the throng. "No, Your Honour. The Venezuelan jungle."

And it was a mud pit, not a mosh pit.

"Hmmm, well let's see if your case is better prepared than your deplorable attire would otherwise indicate." The judge broke into an evil grin.

Another titter.

Fuck you. Fuck you all. I'll show you.

"Your Honour," Phillip said, taking the chance to glance around him. He was relieved to see Tokio Jones sitting beside him. She held her Aurora Special fountain pen in her well-manicured right hand. The pen was one of the most valuable in the superpower world. Anything written with it was visible only to its author and anyone the author wanted to read it. Her nail polish featured little yellow flames. He hoped she was in a fiery mood. He glanced as she scrawled a note.

First witness is his uncle, Gascon Paradis.

"Counsellor?" Judge Sexby sounded annoyed.

Phillip glanced up from Tokio's note. Nobody had arrived from the defence side yet, so he had a few moments to compose his thoughts. Who the hell had scheduled Gascon Paradis to appear first? Talk about jumping in the deep end of the pool with rocks tied around his ankles. He felt the weight of the collective stares around the courtroom.

"Your Honour, the defence team has yet to arrive." Phillip hoped they'd take a while.

Judge Sexby shifted in his massive chair at the head of the court. The slight movement sent licks of flames shooting along the back of the blackened chair. Phillip saw scorch marks along the wooden grain. As a prosecuting attorney, he'd been the cause of a few of the burns. He wasn't about to break his record now.

"That's never stopped us before," Judge Sexby boomed. "Proceed."

"But, Your Honour, Daine Paradis is a mortal who until this morning had no idea he possessed supernatural powers. He doesn't even have a defence attorney."

"How do you know this?" The Judge's tone was frigid, the little yellow flames licking across his seat back popping and hissing. The bailiff beside him jumped away from the chair.

"I spoke to him and a few of his defence witnesses." Phillip frowned. It looked as if the judge had an agenda.

"Really." It was a statement, not a question. There was a fresh spark, a kind of interest, in Judge Sexby's eyes. He was either about to smote Phillip right there in his bare feet, or he was about to give him a few extra minutes.

"Your Honour, considering the nature of the charges, the defendant, Mr. Paradis, should be here to listen to the charges as they're read. He also—"

"I believe he's already in the tunnel, counsellor, so save the pretty speeches for your opening remarks." Disdain dripped from the judge's words.

A few people twittered, but most of them had already craned their necks towards the metal bars guarding the Tunnel of Doom. It was from there that the accused started and ended their trials. The metal bars lifted and the red Fire doors clanged open. If Phillip hadn't been so worried about Daine, he would have rolled his eyes at the Fire bells clanging, the intense flames shooting up around the courtroom as two armed guards escorted Daine into the courtroom.

Even in borrowed clothing and with a look of terror on his face, Daine was a handsome man. His pain was heartbreaking. His gaze darted around the room. The flames rocking up the walls increased a notch.

Judge Sexby is such a show-off.

Daine's gaze fell on Phillip's face. Phillip winked at him then bent his head to shuffle the papers Tokio had just placed in front of him. Daine walked stiffly, one of the guards jabbing him in the back with his lance.

Man, they're a pair of hams, too.

"Your Honour, is it necessary for the guards to be manhandling the defendant?" Phillip asked.

"Not necessary, but it amuses the court," Judge Sexby intoned, making a few court watchers laugh. It was probably not the judge's finest moment. The terror on Daine's face was palpable and not a single juror was smiling.

"Ease up, Artair," Judge Sexby finally said.

Where had this pair of misfits come from? Phillip stared at the fur capes on the two guards who looked like a pair of Neanderthals straight out of Central Casting.

Artair flashed a look of fury at Judge Sexby. Fire danced in his eyes. Phillip began to worry. Artair was a true Fire-Keeper. He would happily incinerate Daine were he to be judged as guilty.

It won't come to that. He put on this whole circus to scare Daine, to intimidate him.

"We're waiting, Counsellor," Judge Sexby boomed.

"The defendant hasn't reached the defence table yet, Your Honour." Phillip was going to push for them to stick within the rules.

"He's taking an awfully long time." Judge Sexby sounded crotchety.

This was true. Daine shuffled in baby steps. Phillip caught him wincing and glanced down in horror. He saw that his lover's feet were in leg irons.

"Your Honour, if the guards could remove the shackles on the defendant, I'm certain that his progress would be much faster." Phillip barely contained his anger.

"You don't think he's a flight risk?" the judge asked.

"Not even without leg irons," Phillip said.

He caught Daine's traumatised gaze. He wondered how the man would ever get over such a harrowing experience.

And he's innocent.

People were whispering now. A bit of razzle-dazzle was one thing. Obvious cruelty was another.

The judge kept silent.

Daine seemed to be limping.

"Mr. Paradis is still innocent until proven guilty, Your Honour," Phillip said.

"Oh, all right." Judge Sexby waved his hand and Daine's steps became swifter.

He shot Phillip a grateful look and moved to the table Phillip pointed out to him.

"Remove the handcuffs," Phillip told the guards. Neither man moved a muscle. "Your Honour —"

Another wave of the judge's hand and the handcuffs were gone. Daine rubbed first one wrist, then the other, the marks from the cuffs still evident on his skin.

"Proceed." Judge Sexby was so angry that smoke whisked out of his ears.

Daine stared at the man.

Phillip felt a rush of movement by his side. Declan had joined Tokio. Over his shoulder he could see that the courtroom was tightly packed. He picked out Mr. Arden in the crowd, who nodded to him.

"Your Honour, at this time, I would like to call the defence attorney to join Mr. Paradis at his table." Phillip needed to know who he was working with.

"Where is your attorney?" Judge Sexby asked Daine. He shifted in his chair again. Boy, was he in a pissy mood or what?

"I don't have one, Your...er...Honour."

"Yes, he does." A female voice came from the back of the court.

All heads turned and Phillip's heart sank. It was, inexplicable as it seemed, Cairo, Daine's pink-haired, flaky, unreliable assistant and icing-maker from the bakery.

"Oh my God," Daine said, his head sinking into his hands.

* * * *

Daine sat in his chair, pain radiating down his hip to his feet. The guard had jabbed him the entire time he'd walked from the horrible tunnel. He felt a trickle of blood shoot down to his bare foot.

I'm sitting in a weird-ass courtroom with Cairo as my defence attorney. Holy shit. Somebody shoot me now. Just get it over with. I'm commando in borrowed jeans and I've got no shoes on, and a guard who looks like Attila the Hun with the personality of a dozen serial killers is staring at me. And what the fuck is with all this fire? Shit! Even the ground feels hot!

He lifted his feet and noticed a few people around him staring — others were also getting squirrely in their seats. The courtroom felt like a towering inferno. He wiped sweat from his brow with the back of his hand.

"Your Honour," Cairo said, "If it pleases the court, I'm here to represent Mr. Paradis."

"No, you're not," Daine shouted. "You're the flakiest shop assistant I ever had! You're not representing me in anything. You — you'll send me to the guillotine!"

The courtroom erupted in laughter.

She turned and gave Daine a tight smile. The expression on her face was one he'd never seen before on her usual hippy-dippy countenance.

"Control your client, please, Ms. Fire." The judge was grinning.

"Fire?" Daine stared at her. "I thought your family name was Rhodes."

"I was incognito." Cairo grimaced.

"Of course you were." Daine shook his head. His reality, or what he'd thought of as reality, was quickly going up in flames. "Any relation to Christopher?"

"Sister," she said, her voice so soft he barely caught the word.

"Sorry, Your Honour," Daine said.

"Shut up," Judge Sexby shouted.

Daine shut up. He glanced over at Phillip's table and caught his lover's stricken expression.

I should just tie myself to the stake right now. This is so not going well...

"Your Honour, I believe the prosecution plans to call its first witness, if the attorney is ready...sometime soon?" Cairo swivelled her head towards Phillip.

"I'm waiting for you to be sworn in," Phillip said.

Cairo looked flustered. "Oh. Yeah. Right."

A bailiff rushed over with a large, leather-bound book. Cairo put her left hand on it, raising her right hand.

"I do solemnly swear to uphold the truth and power of the Fire Court. So mote it be." Cairo pulled back her hand.

The bailiff held the book towards Daine.

"What is it? What's in the book?" Daine asked.

"The Fire-Bible, of course," Cairo said, looking shocked.

"You've never seen one before?" Judge Sexby asked.

Daine shook his head. The book had wisps of smoke streaming from it. He could feel the heat from here. Was it even safe to touch?

"Was that a response, Mr. Paradis?" The judge leant forward.

"Er...no, Your Honour." Daine wasn't trying to be difficult, but he didn't know what was going on here. He wanted to avoid making more mistakes.

"No, that wasn't a response, or no, you've never seen a Fire-Bible before?" The judge, at least, seemed to be having a good time, if his widening grin was any indication.

"Um...both," Daine said. He was now so hot his brain seemed scrambled. "I've never seen one before." He added, "Your Honour," as sweat streamed from his hairline into his collar.

"Take your oath," Cairo said and Daine did, his hand burning as he touched the bible. He felt as if the tome sent some invisible truth-seeking spirit into his body as he repeated the same words Cairo had just recited.

Phillip was next, then the courtroom hushed as the bailiff raced to shelve the steaming book.

"Court be seated," another bailiff said.

"Don't worry," Cairo said, when they took a seat and waited for Phillip to begin. "I have just as much power as my brother, but without the fancy title."

"How many people have you defended before?" Daine prayed she was as experienced at this as at making icing.

She looked him right in the eye. "You're my first."

Phillip stood, his damp hair sticking in sexy tendrils around his face and neck. He too was barefoot, and Daine could see him lifting first one foot from the hot floor then the other.

"Your Honour, as you know, we are here today to examine whether or not Daine Paradis abused his superpowers in the course of conducting his business as owner and operator of Fabulous Cupcakes, an established bakery located at 2200 Fulton Street in San Francisco." Phillip looked magnificent, even in his casual clothes.

Seeing him in a robe and full regalia would probably make Daine come on the spot. He blushed. *Shit, I've got to pull myself together. My life's at stake here.*

"Proceed." Judge Sexby's pronouncement seemed to cool things down a notch.

Daine stole a glance at his palm that had rested on the Fire-Bible. It was red but there were no blisters, in spite of the searing pain he'd felt.

"My first witness is Mr. Gascon Paradis, the defendant's uncle." Cairo's voice sounded more confident than it had ever been before.

Daine hadn't seen his uncle in two years and the nature of their estrangement still caused him heartache. As a kid, Uncle Gascon had been his favourite adult. He'd taken Daine to the zoo, to the movies and had even let him back Gascon's Lincoln Continental out of his driveway in the mornings.

What the hell is he going to say? Is he gonna crucify me? Do they hang people in a Fire Court? With his luck, he was going to end up at the stake.

Uncle Gascon walked towards the witness box with an unsteady gait. He was limping heavily. He'd always looked remarkably like his brother, Marcel, but he'd aged badly over the last few years. Bitterness etched his features and a ribbon of grey had taken over his hairline like a one-inch headband around the front. The rest of his head was still the same blond thatch of Paradis hair. He stood in the witness box, took his oath and asked for a glass of water. A bailiff brought him one and he sat, slugging the liquid down, gripping the glass with a shaky hand.

"Are you ill, Mr. Paradis?" Phillip asked.

"No. I have multiple sclerosis." Uncle Gascon's voice was weak.

"I'm sorry to hear that. Are you well enough to give evidence here today?" Phillip looked hopeful.

"My brain still works, if that's what you mean." Uncle Gascon scowled.

"No, I'm asking if you are physically well enough to be here." Phillip smiled, but it looked forced.

"If you get on with it, we'll both find out." Uncle Gascon gripped the edges of the witness box.

The jurors stared at Uncle Gascon.

Man, when had he become such a grouch?

Daine caught his uncle's gaze and was surprised at the look of hatred in the man's eyes.

"Then I won't waste time with softball questions, Mr. Paradis. According to my staff, you're the one who brought this action against your nephew. In a preliminary interview, you indicated that Daine Paradis was abusing his superpowers to further his career and bring about the success of his bakery. May I ask what makes you think he did this?" Phillip's outward calm was deceptive. His eyes told a very different story.

"I don't think it. I know it." Uncle Gascon looked triumphant.

Daine felt his back teeth grinding in his jaw. His uncle hadn't seen him in years! How would he know anything?

"What evidence do you have to prove this allegation?" Phillip tilted his head.

"Have you ever seen the lines outside his store?" Uncle Gascon pointed at Daine, as if wanting to make sure everyone knew whom he was talking about.

Some court watchers laughed, but Daine noticed the jurors watching his uncle intently. For the first time, Daine breathed a little easier and took a closer look at them all. They were truly intimidating, and he found himself shrinking, even though Phillip had told him not to let them scare him.

He caught the gaze of a tall, handsome, strapping man who stared at him. Uh-oh. He wondered if this was the Mage of Berwick his father had mentioned.

"What does this prove? Bakeries and cafés quite frequently have lines outside them," Phillip said.

Daine returned his attention to the proceedings, even though he found himself entranced by a pair of female twins in long, flowing red robes sitting in the jurors' box.

"All day long?" Uncle Gascon responded. "Don't people work anymore?"

Phillip waited for the twittering in the court to die down.

"According to the latest economic figures, no, they don't," Phillip said, and people laughed.

Daine noticed that even the judge smiled.

"Well, let me tell you, it's unnatural. That's what it is," Uncle Gascon said.

"Perhaps the long lines speak more to his gifts in the kitchen, maybe even the lack of able store staff, rather than to the use of superpowers?" Phillip asked.

"Hey, I object to that," Cairo shot back.

"Your Honour, it's a reasonable question," Phillip retorted.

"Overruled." Judge Sexby shot Cairo a dark look.

Phillip continued. "Mr. Paradis, have you been inside the bakery —"

"Of course I've been inside the bakery. My brother owned it until my nephew coerced him into giving it to him." Uncle Gascon's knuckles turned white as he gripped the edge of the witness box more tightly.

Daine wanted to leap to his feet in protest. He was surprised to find Cairo's hand on his arm. It was a feather-light touch, but enough to calm him.

"How did he coerce him?" Phillip asked.

Uncle Gascon shrugged. "How do I know? I have no idea what combination of powers and tricks he used."

Phillip paused. Daine watched him take a piece of paper out of a stack on his table, his gaze remaining on Uncle Gascon.

"Is it not true that you haven't been inside the bakery for at least three years — ever since your nephew took the business over, in fact?" Phillip stared at Uncle Gascon as though willing him to speak the truth.

"Well, yes, but I've walked past. And...I have spies. People tell me they try one of his cupcakes and it's like magic. They forget all their troubles." Uncle Gascon looked around the courtroom, probably expecting applause. None was forthcoming.

"Mr. Paradis, have you ever tried one of your nephew's cupcakes?" Phillip licked his lips, which made Daine grin.

"What's that got to do with anything?"

"Have you ever tried them?"

Uncle Gascon nodded slowly. "Yes, I've tried them."

"When?" Phillip looked incredulous.

His uncle shifted in his seat. Daine wondered if it was a hot seat.

"When he was a little boy." Uncle Gascon's voice was a lot softer than before.

"So he liked to bake even when he was a child?" Phillip smiled.

Uncle Gascon was silent for a moment. "Yes," he said, finally.

"Was he a good baker?"

"The best. I taught him everything I know."

"Did that include the misuse of superpowers?" Phillip's lips twitched.

"Yes—I mean, no. Never. You're confusing me." Uncle Gascon let go of the edges of the witness box and retreated onto his chair.

"So, it's your testimony that Daine Paradis had a knack for baking even when he was a child and you admit that he wasn't using superpowers then. But you assert long lines outside his bakery as a sign of superpower abuse?" Phillip raised his eyebrows.

"Yes, yes!"

"Mr. Paradis, is it not true that, as a possessor of superpowers, one could conjure quicker staff—no offence, Ms. Fire—"

"Some taken," Cairo shot back.

" —and create a way of having no lines?"

"Well, yes…I suppose…if he knew he had the power." Uncle Gascon looked doubtful.

"Ah. But I thought the whole reason you brought this action against your nephew was because he knowingly abused his powers." Phillip was clearly having a hard time stopping his laughter.

"Well, I…look, he just won the Annual Cupcake Competition this year. With his relative lack of experience versus some of the other contestants, what do you call that?" Uncle Gascon leant forwards.

"Talent, perhaps? Possibly hard work?" Phillip paused to let the words sink in. "Nothing further, Your Honour. Your witness, Ms. Fire."

"Thanks, Phil." Cairo grinned.

Daine saw the expression on Phillip's face. He didn't know his lover all that well but could see *Phil* wasn't his choice of nickname.

"Mr. Paradis, can you describe the circumstances surrounding your estrangement with your nephew?" Cairo looked relaxed and comfortable.

Clearly, even though this was her first time in the Fire Court, she was more at home here than in the bakery. *Lucky me!*

"Like I said before, he coerced my brother into giving him the business." Uncle Gascon grimaced.

"Was there money involved in the transaction?"

"What's that got to do with anything?"

"I think it has everything to do with it. Are you aware of Daine Paradis offering his father money for the business?" Cairo wasn't going to let go.

Good!

"Yes." Uncle Gascon looked like he wanted to fly across the room and strangle Cairo.

"Do you know if he paid the amount offered?"

"I have no idea."

"According to my records, he paid his father every cent he owed him. He made regular deposits via wire transfer to a bank account in Caracas, Venezuela." Cairo held up some sheets.

Uncle Gascon didn't reply, his lips were pressed together tightly.

"If Mr. Paradis had indeed coerced his father, would he have needed to make these payments?" Cairo's look of innocence was priceless. Maybe she should have been an actress.

"He needed to make it look good."

"Oh, come on." Cairo shook her head. "Just for the record, Mr. Paradis, how much did *you* offer your brother for the business?"

Uncle Gascon hesitated a moment before whispering, "Nothing."

"Nothing further for this witness, Your Honour." Cairo barely suppressed a grin.

"Redirect," Phillip said.

He held up a red envelope. "Ever seen one of these before?"

Uncle Gascon started to shake in his chair.

"Is it true that, after you filed a complaint against your nephew, you made sure he never saw a single official summons in the hopes of ambushing him with a court date?"

"Never!" Uncle Gascon wheezed and turned purple and red.

"Every picture tells a story, they say." Phillip held up a photograph. "You were spotted at 2.35 a.m. last week by a bank security camera, removing a court summons very much like this one. Care to explain why, Mr. Paradis?"

Uncle Gascon coughed and spluttered, seeming to be in acute respiratory distress. The bailiff brought him more water and his uncle made a big production of swallowing a couple of nasty-looking pills. Daine tried hard not to feel resentful about his uncle's allegations. He was also surprised at how good Cairo was in the courtroom.

Maybe I'm dreaming and I'll wake up and find all this is a horrible nightmare.

Chapter Ten

Daine watched with pride as Phillip rose. His lover stood straight and tall.

"Mr. Paradis, is it not true that you contacted your brother, the defendant's father, six months ago asking him for money to help settle a gambling debt?" Phillip picked up a set of documents from his table.

Uncle Gascon stared at him. "Who told you that?"

"You just did. Have you seen or spoken to your nephew at all since he took over the bakery?"

"No."

"But you've been outside it, observing long lines."

"Yes."

"Why?" Phillip managed to look honestly interested.

Uncle Gascon frowned and looked around, as if seeking help.

"Do you need more time to think about your answer?" Phillip asked.

The courtroom tittered again.

"No. I just don't understand the question." Uncle Gascon shook his head, as if he really had trouble getting the point.

"Oh, I'm talking about sabotage. I'm referring specifically to sending your new wife in there posing as a customer, ordering a cupcake, then calling the health department complaining of food poisoning." Phillip put both hands on his table and leant forward.

"I...er..." Uncle Gascon turned a very bright shade of red.

The lemon cake lady? Oh man... Daine's teeth started grinding again. He had to force himself to stop.

"Isn't it also true you diverted shipments of ordered foodstuffs away from his business seventeen times in the last three months?" Phillip had barely glanced at his papers.

"It wasn't me!" Uncle Gascon's eyes widened.

"Your cell phone records prove otherwise." Phillip held up a sheaf of papers. "Your Honour, I have a wealth of evidence here we might as well start entering into the official record. The cell phone records of this witness will be entered as Fire People's Exhibit A."

"So noted," Judge Sexby said.

A bailiff took the paperwork out of Phillip's hand.

"Mr. Paradis, is it not also true that you erroneously reported Daine's kitchen staff as illegal, undocumented immigrant workers to the Immigration and Naturalisation Service?" Phillip was on a roll now.

"I...er..."

"I'll take that as a yes. Nothing further, Your Honour." Phillip sat down, smiling.

Daine watched him confer with the woman at his side. He felt a small measure of relief. Phillip seemed to be doing a better job of proving his innocence than his guilt.

He started to relax a little until the next witness was called. To his utter dismay, it was his roommate, Ben. Daine hadn't seen Ben, or his lover Steve, in weeks…and now the guy was here giving evidence against him. Ben looked as bewildered as Daine felt.

Phillip stood. "Please state your name for the record."

"Benjamin Silberstein." Ben's grin was loopy and infectious.

"What is your relationship to the defendant?"

"He's my best friend and my roommate." He gave a little finger wave to Daine, who waved back until he realised the judge was frowning at him.

"Mr. Silberstein, how well do you know the defendant?" Phillip hadn't smiled at all.

"Very well. We went to school together from the time we were eight years old." Ben was still grinning.

"What was he like?"

"A total dork."

Oh, geez, thanks a lot. Daine rubbed his hand over his face.

"I mean that in a nice way. Say…where am I?" Ben looked around, clearly confused.

"You're in court, Mr. Silberstein." Phillip cleared his throat.

"That musta been some wacky tobaccy I smoked tonight." Ben swayed and gripped the edge of the witness box for support.

"Don't worry, Mr. Silberstein, you won't remember any of this. You'll just think you blacked out." Phillip grinned.

Ben blinked. "Oh, cool."

Cool. Geez, Louise.

"Mr. Silberstein, why do you say Daine Paradis was a dork?" Phillip had a hard time suppressing his grin.

I'll get you for that!

"He liked to cook. He was so gay, even when we were kids!" Ben laughed.

Double thanks, dickhead.

"Do you recall him ever making a bad meal?"

"Mmm…nope. Matter of fact, he was scary good. Say, is your chair on fire?" He swung sideways to stare at Judge Sexby.

"Yes," the judge said.

"Wicked cool, dude." Ben raised an unsteady hand, attempting a thumbs-up.

Oh, my God. What did they give him? He sounds like a frickin' dufus.

"Thanks." Judge Sexby grinned at Ben, surprising Daine.

"Your witness," Phillip said, sending the balance of power over to Cairo.

"No questions, Your Honour." Cairo smiled tightly.

They questioned a couple of Daine's customers, two kitchen hands and even the owner of the restaurant two doors down from Fabulous Cupcakes, who spoke glowingly of Daine's community-mindedness.

He did feel a qualm of anxiety when Lilly, his newest employee, took the stand. At least in her bewilderment she didn't sound like a lunatic…until she began staring at the judge.

"Your Honour," she said. "I seriously, *seriously*, like your boots."

"I have two more witnesses, Your Honour," Phillip said.

"Continue." Judge Sexby waved his hand and Lilly vanished from her seat.

"At this time, I'd like to bring Cairo Fire to the witness stand." Phillip was clearly focussed on bringing this to a dignified end.

Cairo rushed to the witness box. She grinned and waved at the jurors and stood, taking her oath. She touched her hair. It reminded Daine of cotton candy.

"Ms. Fire, can you please tell me why you took the job at Fabulous Cupcakes?" Phillip, once again, managed to look honestly interested.

Maybe he was. Daine certainly wanted to know the answer to that question.

"To be honest, I took it because I'd heard he was good and my brother wanted to have some news about him to tell his father." She shrugged. "So I worked there and kind of kept an eye on him and reported back to my brother."

"What is your brother's name?"

"Christopher Fire."

A roar went up in the crowd.

"A Magus banned by this court." Judge Sexby banged his gavel.

"He abdicated," Cairo said, her cheeks reddening. "He...he was railroaded!"

"Ms. Fire, you'll keep your responses to the questions, please." Phillip's tone was stern.

She pulled a face. "Fine."

"When and why did you begin sabotaging Fabulous Cupcakes?"

"As soon as you asked me to." Cairo looked confused.

Daine gasped. Phillip's head turned right to him, his expression one of horror. Then it swivelled back to Cairo.

"*I* asked you to do this, Ms. Fire?" Phillip's eyebrows were trying to hide under his hair.

"Well, not you. Mr. Arden did." Cairo shrugged, as if this made no difference.

It meant the world to Daine.

"With what purpose?" Phillip frowned.

"To see if Daine used superpowers to rectify big or small catastrophes."

"And did he?" Phillip leant forward.

Her eyes widened. "Not once."

"In your opinion, as a staffer who worked side by side with him every day, did you observe any misuse of superpowers?" Phillip looked relieved.

"None. It was almost painful to watch. I truly don't think he knew he had any powers at all." She looked at Daine. "Sorry I was such a bitch, doll."

Daine shrugged.

"Your Honour," Phillip said, over the courtroom laughter, "at this time, I'd like to bring out my final witness."

Phillip took a deep breath. "I'd like to bring retired justice Marcel Paradis to the stand."

Daine felt a lump form in his throat. There was an awed silence. His father appeared from the tunnel looking amazing in his red Fire robes. The entire courtroom stood.

They love him, Daine thought. *They really, really love him.*

* * * *

Daine noticed Christopher walking behind his father. He came and took a seat beside Daine, his hand reaching over to his for a brief squeeze.

His father took the stand and dazzled everyone by bringing the Fire-Bible to himself with a slight movement of one finger.

"Is he hot, or what?" Christopher asked him.

Daine stared at his father.

Phillip began. "Mr. Paradis, please explain your long absence from this court."

"I was asked to adjudicate three years ago on the matter of the Fire People versus Christopher Fire." Daine's father looked a lot more relaxed now that he was back on familiar ground.

"And what happened?"

"I had to recuse myself since he was my lover." Daine's father looked straight at Phillip.

Daine expected a lot of noise but instead, silence greeted the revelation.

"Isn't it true that the Fire Court approached you, asking you to intervene on its behalf to coerce your son to take his rightful place as a Magus in the cooking realm?" Phillip asked.

"Yes."

"How did you respond?"

"I declined."

"Why?"

"I knew my son had worked hard and loved his job at the bakery. I'm proud of my boy. I wasn't going to sabotage that. I'll also admit...I was frightened." A brief look of uncertainty crossed his father's face, but was gone just as quickly.

"Frightened? Why?" Phillip tilted his head.

"Superpowers have brought nothing but misery to me." Daine's father looked bitter for a moment.

There was a murmur in the room.

"Do you still feel that?"

"No. Listening to all the people who spoke so glowingly of my son today, I know he has superpowers, but I also know he only found out today. He couldn't have used them before because he wasn't aware he had any. I also miss my days as a jurist. I think...I think my biggest fear is that my failings have visited themselves on him. I can't bear that. I can't bear to think of him losing everything for my foolish weakness."

"Your Honour, the prosecution rests."

That's it? Shit! Do I live or die?

Cairo stood and tossed some questions to his father, who handled them easily. On redirect from Phillip, his father admitted that he regretted not fighting in the court system for his job, or for Christopher's title as Magus.

The courtroom buzzed when the jurors left to deliberate.

"What do you think?" Daine asked his father, Cairo and Christopher as they waited in a small anteroom.

"Phillip didn't try to skewer you once," his father said. Daine looked at his old man and hugged him.

A bailiff came to the door.

"The jurors have a verdict," he said.

"Holy crap, that was fast," Cairo said.

"Have faith," Christopher said. They returned in a small huddle to the courtroom.

Daine stood, his father beside him. Daine's legs trembled but he had to think positive. The moments it took the bailiff to carry the note from the juror's foreman to the judge and for Judge Sexby to check over the contents before facing the courtroom were the longest of his life.

Judge Sexby nodded to the jurors.

"On the charges of misuse of superpowers, the jurors find the defendant not guilty."

There was a whoop of joy and everyone around him burst into applause.

Judge Sexby shouted over the noise.

"Daine Paradis, do you accept your rightful duty as a Magus of the Fire House?"

"Yes, Your Honour, on one condition." Daine felt the shocked faces turning on him.

"What is that?" the judge asked him, narrowing his eyes.

"I want my father and his husband to have their powers restored. Christopher and I have a lot of baking to do." Daine wasn't going to back down, even though his stomach fluttered at the thought of the power the judge could unleash.

The judge smiled. *Thank God!*

"Mr. Fire, if this condition is granted, there is to be no funny business from you." Judge Sexby looked stern again.

"Yes, Your Honour." Christopher nodded. Then aside to Daine, he said, "You make one little mistake and sheesh…"

People clapped Daine's back. He was aware of Phillip hovering but couldn't get near him. His father seemed younger and taller as he greeted well-wishers.

When Daine turned, Phillip was gone.

Christopher touched Daine's shoulder. "So, how does it feel to be the official cake guy?"

Daine laughed. "Better than being in the tunnel with Heckyl and Jeckyl."

"Oh, yeah, they're a pair of tools, aren't they? Hey, don't you think my sister did an awesome job as your attorney?" Christopher looked proud.

"I sure do." In spite of all the nonsense she'd put him through these past few months as his assistant, he was grateful to her.

He hugged her, then asked when she was coming back to work with him.

"I'm not. I'm opening my own bakery. Cairo's Cakes."

"Oh," he said, taken aback.

As soon as she'd drifted away, Christopher muttered, "I give it six months."

* * * *

Phillip sat at his desk, head in his hands. He should have been celebrating Daine's victory, and he was grateful that everything had worked out so well. He really was. But he couldn't get into the spirit of it. His boss was still nowhere to be seen, and with everything that had gone down, and him basically botching his job as a prosecuting attorney, Phillip might not even have a job anymore.

That wasn't the worst of it, though. He missed Daine. His lover had looked so relieved and happy when the jurors returned their verdict, it still made Phillip smile. He'd wanted to take him into his arms and kiss him, but he hadn't been able to get close enough to him in the courtroom, not even for a handshake. All the well-wishers had made sure of that.

Was it always going to be like that? Daine was an important person now, a veritable superpower VIP. As a Fire Magus, one of only five in the Fire House, was he even going to be interested in Phillip anymore? Daine could have any man he wanted, there was no reason he would stick with Phillip.

He groaned. He wanted Daine with every fibre of his being.

"Phillip?" Daine's voice sounded hesitant.

Phillip's head flew up and he had to grip the desk's edge to avoid falling off his chair. Daine stood right there in his office doorway, still barefoot and in his borrowed clothes, looking adorable.

"Daine!" Phillip had never felt relief like this. Daine was here, and he didn't look like he was about to dump him. Maybe not all was lost.

"I'm sorry to bother you at the office, but I need to know…" Daine gripped the door frame and closed his eyes.

Phillip jumped up, ran around the desk and took his lover into his arms faster than a bush fire spreads in the dry season. Daine sagged against him, holding onto him with enough force to squeeze the air out of his lungs.

Phillip didn't mind.

"You're not bothering me, whatever gave you that idea?" He moved Daine fully into his office and closed the door, locking it while he was at it.

"I don't know." Daine's voice was muffled against Phillip's chest, his hot breath warming him even through the fabric of his shirt. "You were gone from the courtroom so quickly, I wasn't sure you wanted anything to do with me anymore."

Phillip knew laughing was probably the wrong reaction but he couldn't stop the happy sound from escaping. They were quite the pair.

"I'm sorry you think that's funny." Daine lifted his head, his eyes suspiciously bright as he tried to pull back.

"I wasn't laughing because I think it's funny, sweetheart." Phillip refused to let Daine go and started walking them towards the sofa. He needed to sit down to deal with this rollercoaster of emotions.

"You weren't?" Hope blossomed in Daine's eyes as they sat down as close to each other as Phillip could manage.

"No, I was laughing because I'd been afraid of the same thing and I was so happy to hear that I was wrong." Phillip took Daine's hands in his and squeezed them.

"You were afraid I didn't want anything to do with you? Why?" Daine's eyes were wide.

"You're an important Magus now, and I'm just a lawyer." Phillip shrugged. "One who went against you in court, no less."

"First of all, forget about the Magus stuff. I have no idea what that means anyway, and they can have the title back in a second, if it comes between us." Daine looked fierce, brows furrowed and movements controlled. "As for you being a lawyer, I'm damned grateful for that."

"You are?" Phillip dared to breathe again.

"Yeah, you saved my butt in there. Maybe you were supposed to be the prosecutor, but all I saw you do once the trial got started was make sure everyone saw my innocence. It was amazing." Daine grinned and gave him a much too brief kiss on the cheek. "Thank you."

"You're welcome." Phillip smiled. "I just hope my bosses will be as enthusiastic. After all, as far as they're concerned, I failed."

"Don't worry about them." Daine waived a hand in the air. "If they don't see sense, you can always work in the bakery with Christopher and me."

"Christopher and you, huh?" Phillip pulled back. "Should I be jealous?"

"What?" Daine looked honestly puzzled for a moment.

"Well, he *is* a good-looking man." Phillip had a hard time suppressing his smile.

"Oh, you've noticed that?" Daine grinned. "Baby, he's got nothing on you. Anyway, he's my father's lover, for heaven's sake. What would I want with him?"

"I don't know…" Phillip shrugged.

"I'll tell you what." Daine leant forward so they were close enough for their noses to touch. "If either of us has any time to notice other men from now on, we'll have to come up with a suitable punishment, because it'll mean one or both of us failed at his job."

"What job?" Phillip liked how close Daine was to him now. He could smell his lover's musk and feel the heat of his breath on his skin.

"The job of being a boyfriend, of course." Daine moved back a little. "If you want to be, that is."

"That's the only job I'm really interested in, sweetheart." Phillip pulled Daine back into his arms for a long, tender kiss.

When they came up for air, Daine's eyes were glazed with lust.

"Want you." Daine glanced at the desk.

Really? God, that made him harder than rock.

"You have me, baby." Phillip cupped Daine's neck, pulling him close enough to whisper into his ear. "Anywhere you want me — even on the desk."

"Fuck." Daine turned to insert a leg between Phillip's thighs, pressing his erection against Phillip's thigh in the process. "Please?"

"Anything for you." And it wasn't like it would be a hardship for him.

Daine rubbed his hard cock against Phillip's thigh, clearly desperate for friction. Phillip slid a hand to his lover's ass, kneading the tight muscles. Daine moaned and pushed harder.

"Naked. Now." Phillip let go of Daine to pull off his borrowed shirt, opening his jeans before he got distracted again.

"Huh?" Daine's eyes were hooded, his grip on Phillip's shoulders tight. He was too busy grinding himself into Phillip to do much else.

Phillip took off his lover's T-shirt, then pushed him back so he could get at the man's jeans. Button and zipper were quickly opened and the beautiful cock almost jumped up for joy. Phillip couldn't resist and bent down to lick it from base to tip.

"Shit. Good." Daine pushed his hips up.

Phillip complied, taking the leaking tip into his mouth and sucking for all he was worth. Daine whimpered as he tried to push deeper into Phillip's throat. But that wasn't what he wanted. Well, not this time.

Phillip let go of the hard cock in his mouth, swearing he'd return soon. Daine looked disoriented. Philip got up, held out his hand and pulled Daine with him towards the desk. If they didn't get there now, they'd lose this opportunity because Phillip was more than ready to come.

He pushed Daine's pants down and off before laying him out on the desk, loving the way his lover stretched his arms to grip the other edge. Daine lifted his head and smiled as he bent his knees so he could put his feet up onto the surface, spreading his legs as he went.

Phillip stopped breathing and stared. Daine's cock strained up against the flat belly, stiff with arousal, his heavy ball sac weighed down between his legs. His lover had the most beautiful ass in the world, but with his hole on display like this, the sight was mouth-watering.

"Like what you see?" Daine took his cock in hand and started stroking.

"God, yes." Phillip wanted to plunge right in.

He shook his head to clear his mind. Condom first, then lube. Bending down to his briefcase, he retrieved a foil packet but found no slick stuff anywhere. Fuck! Nonplussed for a moment, he tried to switch his brain back on. Desk drawer! There was always useful stuff in there, and with any luck there'd be hand lotion or something.

He pulled open the drawer with so much force it came off its joints and clattered to the floor. There! A small bottle of hand lotion. He grabbed it and the tissues, depositing both next to Daine's foot. He rose to take the rest of his clothes off. Finally naked, he breathed a sigh of relief. After sheathing himself, he stepped between Daine's legs and smiled down at the gorgeous man.

"Ready?" Phillip took the hand lotion, squirted some onto his fingers and brought them to Daine's tempting hole.

Daine nodded and pushed his hips up. Phillip touched the wrinkled skin, starting to circle the place his cock insisted he needed to be as quickly as possible. Not without preparation, though, He wasn't willing to hurt Daine. Sinking first one finger into the tight channel, then two, he began to scissor them while watching Daine's face for any sign of discomfort.

"More." Daine opened his arms.

Phillip pulled his fingers out of Daine's clenching hole, using the remainder of the lotion to lube his throbbing cock. Carefully positioning the tip against the waiting opening, he started pushing in.

Bending down to move into Daine's arms as he kept pushing in, he sealed their lips into a scorching kiss. Tongues duelling, his arousal started to skyrocket as he bottomed out. There was no way he could have held back. Slowly withdrawing, he thrust back in, making Daine moan and push up against him.

The hard edge of the desk cut into his thighs every time he thrust forward, but he couldn't have cared less. The kiss, combined with the tight heat around his cock, Daine's little whimpers at the back of his throat and the suddenly erotic scent of hand lotion, drove him wild.

He pulled back so he could catch his breath and make sure his lover was with him. He looked at Daine, and suddenly his feelings for this man were overwhelming. Wanting to crawl into him and never leave, he gripped his shoulders and pounded into his ass. Angling his hips just a little, he found what he wanted.

"Phillip!" Daine's eyes widened as he slid his legs around Phillip's waist, bucking up and making his cock head rub their stomachs.

"Baby…" Phillip tightened his grip and continued his deep thrusts into his lover's welcoming channel.

Daine's mouth opened in a silent scream as heat splashed their bellies. His lover's whole body jerked as he emptied his balls between their bodies. That was it. Phillip let go, giving into his need for release. Pleasure raced from his balls up his spine and exploded into a blinding flash of light as he filled the condom.

He collapsed into Daine's welcoming arms and tried to catch his breath. The intoxicating scent of sweat and cum made his cock twitch. Shit, this man did it for him. He lifted his head and smiled into a very satisfied-looking face.

"I don't want to let you go." Daine sounded dreamy. "I think I'm falling for you."

"I feel the same way and I don't want to leave." Phillip kissed Daine's soft lips, savouring the taste of fresh-fucked man.

"Not very practical." Daine giggled. "But I like the sentiment."

"I meant what I said." Phillip pulled back to deal with the condom. "And I want to talk to you about that."

When he was done, he helped Daine up and walked them back to the sofa so they'd be more comfortable.

"How will this work?" Daine sighed as he moved into Phillip's arms. "I mean, I'll be busy with all this Magus training my father has already mentioned. Running the bakery will take a little less time because Christopher will help with that from now on, but there's the business expansion to think of…"

"We can make this work if we really want to." Phillip tightened his embrace. "Whether I still have a job after today or not, I'll help you with the legal side of expanding, if you want. That doesn't worry me."

"So, what does?" Daine looked up at him.

"You and I not spending enough time together." He'd seen what that was like with both of them chasing their careers, and he hadn't liked it. "Which is why I think we should move in together. That way at least we'll know that at the end of the day, we'll see each other."

"Yes!" Daine started peppering his face with kisses, making him laugh. "I love your apartment, it's much closer to the bakery anyway, and with my roommates almost permanently gone there's no reason for me to stay in Nob Hill."

"As long as you keep the one above the bakery," Phillip whispered. "That one will always be special..."

* * * *

A few weeks later...

Daine was working on a special surprise for his lover and had rarely had so much fun. Creating a new cupcake recipe from scratch was still one of his favourite activities. He grinned as he poured the dough into the special tins, watching the final shape grow before his eyes. For this one, the ingredients were almost less important than the look he wanted.

When the baking tray was complete, he pushed it into the pre-heated oven and set the alarm. Time for a cup of coffee.

He leant back in the chair, watching his kitchen staff at work while he let his thoughts drift. Had he ever been happier?

His trial and the initial hubbub around his new status were over and done with, the supernatural world having returned to normal. His father and Christopher had found a house near the beach and had settled in. His father was working on Uncle Gascon's trial and finding out who had helped him. Christopher had settled into Fabulous Cupcakes as if it was his second home, and was beginning to teach him about being a Magus.

Philip had kept his job, fired the stupid assistant who had almost cost Daine his freedom, and was working hard on whatever big case Mr. Arden had now entrusted him with. His lover didn't say much about his work and that was just fine with Daine. He'd moved into Phillip's apartment a few days ago and felt ecstatic.

When the alarm on his oven went, he jumped up. Glancing at his watch as he walked over, he was relieved to see there was just enough time to decorate his surprise, get ready and be in the apartment by the time Phillip arrived to pick him up for their weekly date night.

Done with the decorations, he covered the tray with a towel, said goodbye to his staff and walked past a widely grinning Christopher. The man knew too much for his own good. Never mind—the privacy of his own four walls, once he'd reached the apartment above the bakery, was good enough for him.

A quick shower later, he heard Phillip's key in the lock. Wearing nothing but a towel around his hips, he went to greet his lover.

"Hey, sweetheart." Phillip stood there in his power suit, looking good enough to lick.

"Hi, baby." Daine stepped closer, rubbing himself against Phillip's body. "Are you ready for some fun?"

"With you, always." Phillip kicked the door closed behind him, dropped his briefcase and loosened his tie. "What have you got planned today?"

"It's over here." Daine stepped away and crooked his finger in a follow me gesture as he walked backwards.

"Why am I not surprised?" Phillip laughed and followed, shedding clothes as he went. He was gloriously naked by the time they made it to the daybed.

Daine stepped to the side to reveal his surprise.

Phillip's eyes widened as he took in the penis-shaped work of art on the spread.

"What the hell?" Phillip managed a brief glance at Daine before returning his attention to the mosaic of penis-shaped cupcakes which added up to a big cock, pointing at the window.

Daine had a hard time suppressing his laughter as he watched his lover take it all in. The colourful decorations, cherries prominent among them, were definitely too much. Phillip's lips finally twitched as he turned back to face him.

"Sweetheart, I think you have too much time on your hands." Phillip stepped closer and pulled Daine up against his hard body.

"*Moi*?" Daine tried to look innocent, but the sparkle in Phillip's eyes was irresistible.

"Yes, *toi*." Phillip's smile broke through. "But I love it!"

"I just wanted us to have something to eat after we got busy." Daine grinned.

"Very thoughtful." Phillip took one of the penis-shaped cupcakes and eyed the green icing that made it look like it was covered by a condom. "But I think I may need an appetiser before we make ourselves comfortable on that sexy daybed of yours."

"Not that we need anything to put fire into our love life." Daine took another one of the little confections and licked the icing off.

Phillip's eyes widened, he dropped his cupcake and pulled Daine back into his arms, mashing their lips together in a kiss that curled Daine's toes.

No, they didn't need a thing to make them hotter than hell. The two of them, minus clothes, were more than enough to fan the flames of love.

About the Authors

A.J. Llewellyn

A. J. Llewellyn is the author of over fifty published gay erotic romance novels. He lives in California, but dreams of living in Hawaii. Frequent trips to all the islands, bags of Kona coffee in his fridge and a healthy collection of Hawaiian records keep this writer refueled. A. J. loves male/male erotica, has a passion for all animals (especially the dog, the cat and the turtle). A. J. believes that love is a song best sung out loud.

Serena Yates

I'm a night owl who starts writing when everyone else in my time zone is asleep. I've loved reading all my life and spent most of my childhood with my nose buried in a book. Although I always wanted to be a writer, financial independence came first. Twenty-some years and a successful business career later I took some online writing classes and never looked back. Living and working in seven countries has taught me that there's more than one way to get things done. It has instilled tremendous respect for the many different cultures, beliefs, attitudes and preferences that exist on our planet.

I like exploring those differences in my stories, most of which happen to be romances. My characters have a tendency to want to do their own thing, so I often have to rein them back in. The one thing we all agree on is the desire for a happy ending.

I currently live in the United Kingdom, sharing my house with a vast collection of books. I like reading, traveling, spending time with my nieces and listening to classical music. I have a passion for science and learning new languages.

A.J. Llewellyn and Serena Yates love to hear from readers.

You can find their contact information, website details and author profile pages at http://www.total-e-bound.com.

Total-E-Bound Publishing

www.total-e-bound.com

Take a look at our exciting range of literagasmic™
erotic romance titles and discover pure quality
at Total-E-Bound.